PRAISE FOR Into that forest

'A STRANGE, POWERFUL, ORIGINAL TALE.' *The Sunday Times*

'I WAS COMPLETELY SPELLBOUND.' *Lovereading*

'STRIKINGLY ORIGINAL . . . VIVID.' *The Bookseller*

'A WONDERFUL BOOK, UNLIKE ANYTHING I'VE READ BEFORE.
IT LINGERED WITH ME LONG AFTER TURNING THE FINAL PAGE.'
A Dream of Books

'BOTH JOYFUL AND HEARTBREAKING, NOWRA HAS CREATED A
TRULY EXTRAORDINARY WORLD WHICH IS DIFFICULT TO LEAVE.
IT'S A MAGICAL BOOK.' *Irish Examiner*

'A FANTASTIC TALE.' *Newcastle Journal*

'A BRILLIANT AND EXTRAORDINARY VOICE . . . A BEAUTIFULLY
POIGNANT STORY ABOUT SURVIVAL AND RELATIONSHIPS.'
Mr Ripley's Enchanted Books

'YOU'LL NEVER FORGET IT.' *Readingzone*

'A GORGEOUSLY VIVID IMAGINING OF LIFE IN THE WILD.' *Bookbag*

'ORIGINAL AND MOVING.' *The Lady*

'READS LIKE A TRUE STORY – MOVING AND SHOCKING.'
Lincolnshire Echo

Louis Nowra is a critically acclaimed, multi-award-winning writer of plays, film and TV scripts, non-fiction, memoir and fiction. He was born in Melbourne and lives in Sydney with his wife, Mandy Sayer, also a writer, and their Chihuahua, Coco, and Miniature Pinscher, Basil.

Into that forest

LOUIS NOWRA

EGMONT

EGMONT

We bring stories to life

Into that Forest
First published in Australia 2012
by Allen & Unwin,
83 Alexander Street, Crows Nest NSW 2065, Australia

First published in Great Britain 2012 by Egmont UK Limited
This edition published 2013
by Egmont UK Limited
The Yellow Building, 1 Nicholas Road, London W11 4AN

ISBN 978 1 4052 6717 5

3 5 7 9 10 8 6 4 2

www.egmont.co.uk

A CIP catalogue record for this title is available from the British Library

54620/4

Typeset by Avon DataSet Ltd, Bidford on Avon, Warwickshire
Printed and bound in Great Britain by CPI Group

FSC
MIX
Paper
FSC® C018306

EGMONT

Our story began over a century ago, when seventeen-year-old
Egmont Harald Petersen found a coin in the street. He was on
his way to buy a flyswatter, a small hand-operated printing
machine that he then set up in his tiny apartment.

The coin brought him such good luck that today Egmont has
offices in over 30 countries around the world. And that lucky
coin is still kept at the company's head offices in Denmark.

To Vincent Ward

Me name be Hannah O'Brien and I be seventy-six years old. Me first thing is an apology – me language is bad cos I lost it and had to learn it again. But here's me story and I be glad to tell it before I hop the twig.

I were born in Tasmania, born not in a hospital but here in the backblocks. In this actual house. It is crumbling round me ears now, but the roof hardly leaks and if I chop enough wood I can heat the place when it snows. Though I live here by meself I am not lonely. I got a wedding photograph of me mother and me father when men wore beards and sat down for the picture while me mother wears a wedding dress and stands beside him. And there's

1

me father's harpoon hanging from the living room wall with its cracked wooden handle and rusted blade. Me only new thing is the cabinet with a radio in it which Mr Dixon down at the general store gave me. I can't hack it. There always be mongrel music in it, like it's shouting all the time. Anyway, I'd sooner yabber to meself than listen to those voices inside that box. I reckon I need new curtains, these are a bit dusty and fraying, but they keep out the summer light when it's so strong it hurts me eyes.

I think me uncle built this house. He gave it to me father. It were a present. At that time we were the only house for miles and miles. Me father wanted to live in a place near water – if not the sea, then a river. Me mother liked rivers and so the house were a give-and-take for the both of them. From the verandah we could almost touch the Munro River as it flowed down to the sea. I had no brothers or sisters. I don't know why. There were a problem, I think. I'd hear me mother crying buckets in me father's arms and hear him say, like to a child, *There, there, we got Hannah.*

Me first memories, well, the thing is, and this be strange when I think about it, but me first memories, they are really me father's. Maybe not even his memories, maybe his stories. I'd drop into a swoon of gladness when he come to me bedroom to put me to sleep and he'd tell me 'bout his adventures. He were a whaler and when he came back after travelling the seas, he'd tell me these stories, stories about places and things he'd set eyes on. I s'pose me mind made them me own so I thought it was me, Hannah, in the Philippines and I could see two black men in a boat, the sort hacked out of a log, and they were waiting for a whale shark. When it came, one fisherman jumped out of the boat onto the back of the whale shark and rode it like it were a brumby and at the same time he stabbed it in the back til it croaked. In the South Seas, in water so clear you could see right down to the bottom where queer fish swim, a fisherman jumped into the sea

3

with a banana in his mouth. He spitted bits of the banana at a huge groper which gobbled them up, all the time coming closer and closer til the fisherman caught that big fish in his bare hands. There were another time when me father were at the bow and a sperm whale, big as a house, were harpooned and the whale boat, stuck fast to the wounded whale, were dragged along at a wild speed towards the sun on the horizon til the monster carked it of exhaustion. One time me father were at anchor in Western Australia when he seen a gin on a beach and she were singing a song, an uncanny song like you sing to ghosts, but it called to the whales. One whale, a minke, came to shore sucked in by her song and beached itself like a sacrifice for her. On the Tasmanian coast, near South Bruny, a whale were winched into the flensing yard where a big puncture were cut into the back of the creature and an old man, he crippled with tuberculosis so bad that he walked on all fours, were put into it, like a plug down a hole. He was pulled out half a day later and all the workers were thunderstruck cos this fellow could walk and he was straight-backed. He had been cured.

When me father came home from his voyages, you knew. When me mother and I lived by ourselves everything were quiet, but when me father were in the house there were singing and me mother kept bursting into giggles and me father's footsteps were loud and happy. One time when I were 'bout five he brought back some stuff from inside a whale. He had carved it out from deep inside its spout. It were like a small, grey, ugly sponge. He put it in a jar and sometimes I opened the lid and sniffed it. It half stank of dead, putrid things from the sea but when I got past that stink I smelt perfume, ever so sweet: a rosy, sugary mist. Me father said it were worth more than gold but he never tried to sell it – it were to be me dowry. He had lots of memories of his whaling – there were a harpoon on the wall, baleen always drying on the back verandah, rigging ropes and cutting blades so sharp that when the sun shone on the blades it cut the shine up into thin pieces. People smile when I say that, but I seen it with me own eyes.

His times away growed longer cos whales were harder to find. Once Derwent River were so choked with whales that it were just a matter of going out in a boat and harpooning – you could do it wearing a blindfold, there were so many right whales using the river as a nursery. The people of Hobart used to complain that they couldn't sleep cos of all the whales blowing all the time. That's how many there were, me father said. Now he had to go to all parts of the globe. Me mother and me were close, like sisters, when me father were away. She taught me to read and write. I were very keen on animals, especially Sam the pig. He were as big as a beer barrel and he allowed me to ride him. I spent a lot of time with him, talking to him in grunts and snuffles. I never made fun of him by going *Oink, oink.* Me mother used to get worried. *Why you talking to Sam like he were a person?* But I were lonely being a child in the bush by meself, and, you know, I were just a little girl, but I'd look at Sam as I were talking to him and he'd seem to understand, like he were listening really hard to me.

Cos I liked being outside and playing, I were always dirty and me mother would shake her head and say, *You're grubby or filthy, but never clean, Hannah.* I couldn't help it. If I ate food at the table, some of it would always slide out of the side of me mouth and plop onto me clothes. There's a cobweb across two trees in the back yard, well, I don't know how I do it, but pretty soon I'm wearing it like a hair net. Me hair were always such a mess that me mother shoved a bowl on me head and cut me hair – it were a real basin cut. It didn't bother me. But I must oppose meself here. Sometimes I did feel green with envy when me mum would take the pins out of her hair and let it fall down her back. It made her look like one of those mermaids in me picture books. I still remember her cry of *Oh no, Hannah* when I brung home wounded birds or wallaby joeys or blue-tongues. I were always sad to see animals hurt.

Cos our house were far from any town we didn't see many people. We might get a prospector passing by on his way out west where people said there were mountains of gold in places even the blackfellas had been too scared to live. A few times we had this same bounty hunter (or as we called them, tiger man) sleep in the barn for the night. He got paid for the number of tigers he killed. I forget his name, but he had ginger hair and a beard and stank something terrible because he'd rolled in tiger dung and piss, and he had yellow hands and teeth cos a cigarette were never out of his mouth or fingers. Me mother sticked lavender up her nose when he had tea with us so she didn't have to breathe his pong, but as the tiger man said, he had to smell like his prey so they wouldn't take flight when he came along. He told us how he caught two tiger pups and put them in a hessian bag and, knowing their mother were watching what he was doing from where she were hidden in the tall grass and ferns, he threw the bag into the lake and then walked off like he were leaving, but really he hid himself behind a tree and waited for the mother to rush down to the lake to rescue her pups. And when she did, he shot her. He showed no grief in telling us the story – he were skiting, actually – cos the tigers killed sheep, so many that the farmers cried poor. After he killed the mother he yanked the two pups from the bag and strangled them. When I said I felt sorry for the mother and pups the hunter said yes it were terrible, but either humans starved or the tigers did.

The closest people to us lived three hours away. Mr Carsons were a widower and a sheep farmer. His property were by itself between tarn country and wild bush. The tiger hunter stayed with him a lot and he killed dozens of tigers that ate Mr Carsons' sheep. Mr Carsons had a daughter called Rebecca, though she liked to be called Becky. She were a year and a half older than me. She had no mother. Her mother got sick one day and the next day she were covered in purple sores. While Becky's father were getting the buggy ready to take her to Hobart hospital, Becky found her mother near the shearing shed, naked as the day she were born, scratching at her sores, foaming at the mouth and crying out to Jesus to help the pain stop. Becky called out to her father but when he came the poor woman were gone to God.

I did not see Becky much, maybe ten times in two years, but we were the only girls in me whole world and so when we met we were close cos she were lonely too. She were like her father. He had this air 'bout him, he always seemed to be thinking deep thoughts or were glum like an undertaker. When they visited us they always wore their Sunday best. He'd be wearing a black suit and she'd have a lovely blue or pink dress. Oh yes, do not let me forget this – she always wore a cameo of a beautiful woman, who Becky told me were her mother.

One day when I were 'bout six years old – me dates are fuzzy but you will understand why later – me father, who was back from a long voyage, told us that Becky were coming to stay for two days cos Mr

Carsons were going into Blackwood to buy a new buggy. She had only stayed overnight once – and that was the year before – so me father's news made me shiver with pleasure. I were beside meself on the morning of her coming. I couldn't sit still. I were running through the house, sitting on the verandah chair waiting for them, then, quick as a flash, I'd be down to the track to see if they were coming. I run into me parents' bedroom to ask them again 'bout when Becky were coming and I seen me father tying up me mother in a corset. She never wore them when he were whaling but when he was back home she were never without one. It made her look so beautiful. She walked differently, not walked but glided like she were floating a foot above the ground. I knew it were to please me father and in pleasing him she were always in a daze of happiness.

Then Becky arrived in an old buggy with her father. I were so excited to clap eyes on her. I tingle now, thinking about it. You see, I were an alone kid most of me time with just me mother and maybe

11

me father and Sam, me pig. Becky looked gorgeous in her Sunday best with her long golden hair falling down her back. Oh, how I were jealous of that hair cos I had a basin cut and me hair were black like dirt. Her father only stayed for a short time cos it were a long ride into Blackwood. He said he would be back the next evening to have tea with us and stay overnight.

Me father had plans for a picnic, so while he and me mother got everything ready, I took Becky into me parents' bedroom and I showed her one of me mother's corsets hanging from its stand. It had been made especially for her from baleen me father had got from a whale he harpooned. Becky knew nil 'bout whales and were amazed when I told her 'bout the baleen. That pleased me cos she were smarter and a year older than me and could spell words like *encyclopaedia* and *Tasmania*. Then I dragged her into the living room where I unscrewed the lid of the glass jar and shoved her nose down into it. Her face went all wrinkles when she first smelt the stink, but I told her to keep sniffing and then she smiled cos she could smell the musty, sweet scent. I told her how me father had taken it from inside a whale – and she went *Pooh*. I told her how expensive it were – worth twice as much as gold – cos perfume makers need it for their perfumes.

It were going on late morning when the four of us set out in me father's small boat. Me father had one oar and Becky and I pulled on the other til we were so tired that me mother took over. The water were brittle cold, and so clear you could see the pale pebbles on the bottom. On the river banks forests were real thick and there were no sunlight in them. On the river it were so sunny that me mother, when she were not rowing, held up an umbrella so her skin wouldn't burn. Me skin were already covered with angel kisses so I didn't care but when Becky weren't rowing she sat under me mother's white umbrella so the sun didn't burn her either. When the sun did fall on her it made her blonde hair look like a saint's halo. All the time me father rowed he told us yarns 'bout his whaling adventures. Becky's eyes growed as large as saucers when he told her 'bout a man eaten by a sperm whale. It swallowed him right up but when they killed the whale and cut it open there he was, this fella looking like death but still alive. His black hair were bleached white, he had no top skin left and he were nearly blind. Then me father were telling us how he was going to give up whaling cos there were not many whales left when he cried out, *Look!* Before I could see what he was pointing at I heard me mother say, *Oh my goodness, it's one of those hyenas.*

I turned and there, there on the bank not more than ten yards from us, were a wolf creature with yellow fur and black stripes. It were about the size of a real large dog. I can remember it to this day, cos it were the first one I had ever seen. It had a long muzzle and stripes on its sides like a tiger. The tail were thick and the fur so fine and smooth it were like it didn't have hair. *It's like a wolf,* I heard me mother say and indeed it looked like those wolves

I seen in me fairytale books. It stared at us with huge black eyes, then it opened its jaw real slow til I thought it could swallow a baby. I'll go bail if it were not the most bonny, handsomest thing I ever seen. It were like a magician cast a spell on me. I had heard 'bout these creatures, but nothing prepared me for how noble and strange it looked. It snapped its jaws closed. It sounded like two metal doors slamming shut. Then it sort of loped, taking its time, into the bush and vanished.

I must have said it were beautiful, cos Becky hissed real angry, *They are killers. They kill sheep.* She were so firm about this that I were struck dumb. Me father laughed, thinking she were joshing, but she weren't. As he began to row again, he told us why it were so rare to see them. He said they were like vampires. They came out at night and they drinked blood. Me father were chiacking and it made me laugh, but I were sitting next to Becky and I felt her body shiver all over. I can still feel her body against mine and how her fear gave me goosebumps. She went quiet and only perked up when we found a picnic spot.

We moored against a bank and spread out a blanket on the grass in a clearing. Me mother were radiant. Her face were like a pale moon in the shade of her hat. When I ate a banana I held a bit in me mouth and fed it into me father's gob, pushing it through the strainer of his moustache, like I were one of those fishermen with a banana in his mouth luring a groper. After lunch Becky and me went for a walk. We were so thirsty our tongues were hanging out, so we shook the trunks of saplings and the rainwater, trapped in the leaves after the rain, sprinkled down on us and cooled us. Our clothes were wet with water, but we didn't care. I remember, as if right now, standing in me dripping dress in the spotted light coming through the treetops and seeing me parents kissing under the umbrella as they sat on the blanket. I felt a joy dance through me. Me parents were still in love, we were all happy and I had a friend in Becky. An hour or so later, while

Becky and me were chasing each other through the trees and bushes, I heard me mother calling us to come quick. I looked up. The sky had gone sick all of a sudden. Me father said we better go home cos a storm were brewing.

We raced the storm that were coming out of the west at a quicksticks speed. The wind and the current pushed us along so strong that we didn't have to row and me father used one of the oars as a rudder. The sky fell so dark that it was more like night than day.

Me father yelled above the wind and thunder that he'd try and seek a haven. As the water boiled and foamed we bounced along with me father unable to steer the boat towards the shore. The river were so wild that all we could do were to cling on tight to the sides of the boat or each other as we were flinged back and forward like puppets with no strings. The rain chucked down and we were soaked, so soggy it were like the rain were drilling through our skin into our marrow. There were loud bangs when tree boughs broke and fell into the madcap river. Then we were spun round, caught up in a whirlpool. Becky and I went dizzy and screamed in fear. Out of the corner of me eye I seen a giant tree bough bouncing along the river straight at us. Me mother cried out in terror just before it hit us with a crashing and smashing and the next thing I felt were me stomach plopping into me mouth as the boat went over. Oh me, Oh me . . . I must catch me breath in remembering this – I can still feel me terror and all that water pouring into me gob.

I felt meself pulled under like someone were grabbing me leg. Then I came up again only to see me mother's face full of panic there in front of me for a moment before she vanished under the wild waves. I heard screams and again felt me foot were caught in something like an animal trap. I were yanked under. Somehow as I struggled for breath I pulled me foot free from a snag. The waters of the whirlpool grabbed me and hurled me up again, just as me lungs were bursting and then I seen me father. His face were filled with fear. He were crying out me name. He seen me and went to help when the boat, spinning round and round in the whirlpool, hit him in the back of the head and he sank under the waves. A bough floated past and I grabbed at it but me hands slipped on its greasy surface. I sinked again.

It were suddenly calm under the water and I felt like just letting go cos there were too much panic above me. Then through the churning murk I seen me mother. Her white dress were snagged on a tree bough under the water and she were waving her hands slowly in helpless fright. I wanted to swim to her and pull her free but a current grabbed me and chucked me up to the surface. As I were gasping for air, rain stinged me face. Out of the corner of me eye I seen Becky near the bank spinning slowly in a calm eddy. She were on her back, her eyes closed tight. I didn't know if she were dead or not. A piece of a tree knocked me sideways, away from being sucked into the whirlpool towards the bank. Me arms felt heavy like bags of wet sand. I tried to move them so I could get closer to the shore. It seemed such a long way away but as I reached out to grab a tree root on the bank, something dark and huge suddenly loomed over me. It was a tiger, maybe the very tiger I seen before, and its giant jaws opened as if it were 'bout to take me. I screamed.

It moved back from the edge of the bank. The current hugged me round me waist, like some devil wanting to pull me back out in the middle of the river, and I lunged at another of those tree roots but missed. I were 'bout to let the current carry me where it wanted when the tiger were near me again, its jaw wide open, its eyes like cold fire. It grabbed me wrist in its huge mouth and began to drag me. I didn't feel any pain. Maybe I were past all pain. I let meself give in, and it dragged me onto the muddy bank. Once I were out of the river I lay on the wet, long grass panting and gulping for air til me head spinned and I blanked out.

How long I were unconscious, goodness knows, but when I woke up I were on me back in the same spot. The rain were not so heavy, more like a drizzle. For a few moments as I stared at those dark clouds I thought I had come awake from a bad dream. Then me ears were chock full of the loud noise of water bashing against the bank and I sat up. The river was churning something wild and it were rising and starting to creep onto the bank. I felt damp fur against the back of me neck. I turned round and screamed. The tiger, who must have been brushing up against me back, jumped away in fright. I felt a pain and seen teeth marks on me wrist. I tried to shoo it away. It moved back a couple of steps and stopped. It looked at me like it were confused, like I had hurt it or something. So many things went willy-willy through me mind: Where were me parents? Where were Becky? I felt so alone, so lost that I could not see. By that I mean, everything round me were a blur, everything inside me were a blur of fear and shock. I heard meself crying and moaning, *My oh my, my oh my* . . . I still have nightmares 'bout that time. I still feel like a sharp piece of ice has stabbed me heart real deep. I was filled, filled to the brim with utter baffle and utter loneliness.

It were too much for me and all I could do was to plop down where I stood and stare for a long,

long time at the teeth marks of the tiger on me wrist. I have no idea why I did that – maybe it was because I were in a state of shock, maybe because the teeth marks and the pain they caused was so real that it sort of brang me back to reality, whereas everything round me were a fog of too much to bear or understand. I had no fear, no panic any more. Then from a distance, or so it seemed, I heard me name being called. I looked up and seen Becky. She had a real daze on her face. Her dress were clinging to her and she were splattered with mud. She were getting up from the rock pool where she had been floating. For a few moments she did not see me but turned round and round in a panic, crying out me name, p'raps thinking she were alone. *I'm here*, I called out. She stopped in a mid-turn and her mouth dropped open in amazement as if she couldn't believe I were real. *Hannah, Hannah,* she cried, and ran towards me, slipping and falling and tumbling on the wet rocks and the muddy grass. When she got to me she hugged me so tightly I thought she'd crush me. We fell onto the ground and sat hugging there on the damp earth for a long time, not talking, just watching the angry river, hoping hope against hope that me parents would appear.

We must have sat like this for a long time. It were getting dark when the rain stopped. I felt real hungry. There were nothing to eat, cos the food had drowned in the boat. Our loneliness were as sharp as the cold and damp. Then I began to cry cos I feared that me mother and father were drowned. Becky kissed me and stroked me, telling me that they had been taken downstream and were now like us, plonked on a bank, bone-tired and waiting for help. I wanted to believe her and I did. She were older than me and I had to believe her.

Then Becky stood up, cos she were seized by an idea. Her father were going to meet her this time, this evening, at me house. He would see we weren't there and he'd come looking for us. I thought we'd better try and go home and maybe we would run into Mr Carsons who were looking for us. But Becky said her father had always told her that if she got lost she had to stay where she were and wait for rescue cos lost people died trying to find their way home. I must have complained or said I were hungry cos when I got up to go and find some berries, Becky pulled me back and pointed to the forest near us. I turned to where she were pointing and seen two yonnie-sized black suns looking at us from the bush. It were staring right at us, like trying to burn holes into our skin. I were afeared it would come and drink our blood, but Becky said I were silly and that we should stay in the open so we could see it, just in case it came for us. *But what would we do then?* I said. We didn't know. Becky were shivering with fear of the tiger. She had seen what they did to her father's sheep. We were lonely and scared to the quick. Oh dearie, oh dearie me, we were badly shivering with fear.

That were the last thing I remember before waking up as dawn came. I were shaking badly with the cold and I stood up trying to get some warmth into me by rubbing me arms and legs. As I was doing so I seen the tiger sitting in front of the trees, only thirty yards away. It stared at me and then licked its nipples which were seeping milk spotted with what looked like blood. Becky were already awake and she were staring at the tiger and we were both wondering if we were going to be its breakfast. We were hungry too. And we were scared and we hugged each other looking for signs of me parents. *They're gone*, said Becky. *Gone where?* I asked. *Gone, just gone*, she said. Now I were very afeared. I feared, right into the pit of me stomach, that me mother and me father were drowned. I must have been a right gink cos I started to cry that I were hungry. And I cried for me gone parents. I cried for me utter loneliness.

Maybe it were me wailings that caused the tiger to stand up – like I were annoying it – and walk away a few steps. It sat and looked right back at us, like it were trying to tell us something. I stopped me wailing and it got up again, walked a few steps closer, stopped, sat again and stared at us. *It wants to take us home*, I said. Becky said I were loony. But the more I looked at its black eyes, the more I seen kindness, like the kind look in Sam the pig's eyes when we snuggled up together in the sun on the back verandah. I knew it were saying to us, *Come, I'll take you home. Don't be silly*, said Becky, *we'll wait here for people to find us.* But I knew no one would find us and if the tiger took us home, then we would find me mother and me father there, cos maybe they floated all the way back home. Becky were telling me I was a gink when I heard a giant creaking noise coming from the river, a noise like an enormous door with creaking hinges opening. Becky suddenly grabbed me and hugged me to her chest – hugging me so hard I found it hard to breathe. I struggled against her but she were so strong and then after what seemed like minutes she let me go. I gulped down as much air as I could. Then I seen her face. It were white as a ghost. *What is it?* I said but she only shook her head. The tiger stood up again and moved to the edge of the bush, then it turned round and gave us that stare again. *We're going home*, I said and walked towards it. *Hannah!* I heard her cry. She ran after me, sighing long and hard. *All right, Hannah, let's see if it takes us home.* So we followed it into the bush.

What she didn't tell me til later was why she agreed to come with me and the tiger. She had seen something both terrible and beautiful. She heard that great cracking sound and out of the corner of her eye she had seen this *thing* rise out of the river. That's why she hugged me tight, cos a giant tree came out of the water and caught up in its branches were a woman in white, *like some sort of sprite or angel*, she said later, and it were me mother, her eyes closed, her skin pale as death. As Becky hugged me to her she seen this *thing*, this vision drift by. It were me mother taken by the current downriver towards Becky knew not where. If me mother were dead, she reasoned, me father were too. She knew then we had no hope of rescue. We were lost, and the only thing that could help us were the tiger. And so she reckoned she had no choice but to follow that creature she thought might be a vampire and drink our blood.

The bush were more and more thick and thorns tore at our skin. We were considerable weary trying to follow the tiger. Sometimes it stopped and looked back at us, waiting for us to catch up. Becky got trapped up in a thorny bush and it took us a long time to get her free and when she were she fell down and cried buckets, saying over and over, *It doesn't know where to go!* Me stomach made loud gurgling noises and I said I were hungry which was the truth. Becky got angry with me and then yelled at the tiger, *Go away!* I told her not to scare the creature. She said it wanted to lose us and once we were completely lost, and we were dying of hunger, it would eat us cos it had all been a trap.

As she cried and shouted I looked at the tiger which were in front of us, just sitting there in the bush, sort of half invisible as if its stripes had been swallowed up by the shadows, and I seen its kind eyes. It were waiting for us, tongue hanging out. But it were easier for it to get through the bush than for us, so it took us some time til we could make our way through a mess of trees and bushes to a small clearing covered with dead leaves and twigs. *Maybe we can find our own way home*, Becky said, *cos I don't trust him.* I said it were a bitch, not a he, and she weren't going to eat us, and when I were saying this there were these loud snarling and spitting and hissing noises and suddenly, like some vision that had come out of the hole of hell, this creature jumped at Becky who were in front of me. Its jaws were open wide, its big pink tongue spitting at us. It were a Tassie Devil. We cried out in fright and Becky who was next to it started to run but fell, and lo and behold she starts to sink – right there, before me eyes. The leaves and muck were swallowing her up, like it were quicksand, but it weren't, just this hole of rotting leaves and she sank in it, up to her chest. She were in such a state of shock she didn't cry out, but her eyes got bigger in fright. I tried to help her but I started to drown too, so I crawled back onto real ground. I seen the tiger running round the clearing, stopping every couple of steps to lean out to try and grab Becky. Seeing it made me realise what I had to do. I picked up a dead branch covered in lichens and, lying on me belly, I held it out to Becky. She tried to hold the stick but it were awful slippery and she kept on sinking and then, somehow, she managed to hold on to it and I pulled. I yanked on the stick like there were no tomorrow. As I yanked and yanked I heard a sucking sound as poor Becky come out of the muck, inch by inch – it were so slow – and I were grunting like me pig Sam with effort, and lo and behold she came closer and closer, her mouth filled with rotting leaves, her eyes covered in muck, til I dragged her onto the real earth. Then I collapsed with effort. I could not have done it any more. She lied on the ground gasping, groaning, moaning til she got her breath back. We lay on the ground for some time til she began to say over and over, like some needle stuck in a wax cylinder, *We're lost, we're lost.*

I were younger than her but I knew I had to make a decision and there were only one to make and that were to follow the tiger that were on its haunches just a couple of yards away watching us like a mother hawk with her chicks. *We got to go with it,* I said. *And we stay close behind it cos it knows the safe way.* Becky could only nod cos she were that weary and I think, now that I look back, that she probably thought I had saved her life and she had to trust me. Just as I had to trust the tiger.

So we got up and when we did I laughed and Becky were most offended and asked if I were laughing at her and I said, *No, I be laughing at the both of us.* Cos the day before we were wearing clean white dresses and now they were torn and splattered with muck and dead leaves and our hair thick with mud. Maybe cos I were so close to Sam the pig and could see how it had feelings that I seen the tiger step away when I laughed. It did not like the sound of laughing. *I'm sorry,* I said to it. *It doesn't understand you,* snapped Becky. *Well, I think it does, you gink,* I told her. She got annoyed so that meant she didn't say anything for the next hour or so as we trudged after the tiger through that unruly forest.

We walked and walked. We passed through the forest and moved into more open ferny country where in the distance were snowy mountains. All we had to eat were pinkberries, but they are so tiny that they were nothing but reminders we were hungry. Then we got to the side of a creek when night came and the tiger led us to a place under a ledge and there it sat waiting for us. I were going to sit with it when Becky tugged at me dress. *Don't get so close to it*, she warned but I didn't care. The ledge were safe from rain and wind and there were dried ferns on the floor that looked warm and cosy. I crawled up there. I heard Becky say she would keep guard while I were asleep, but they were the last words I heard. I were so tired that I fell asleep straight away.

When I woke up it were first light. Becky were curled up just under the ledge and she were deep in sleep. I looked round for the tiger and seen it at the creek drinking water. It looked up at me when it heard me move. It seemed like a real friendly dog, so I went down to the creek and drank some water. It sat near me, in touching distance. I wondered if I had cuddled it during the night, I didn't know, but it had a warm smell, like fur rugs left on the floor in front of a log fire. It didn't stink at all. I talked to the tiger like it were Sam or a human and it seemed to understand. It pissed in front of me, as casual as you like, not embarrassed at all. So I didn't feel embarrassed when I needed to go to do me business. I squatted and did what I had to do while I chatted to it. I stood up and it came over and sniffed me piss like dogs do, just to check me out. I were promising to give it some whale meat if it took us home when I heard Becky call out from under the ledge, asking what I were doing. *We're having a natter,* I said. On hearing Becky's voice the tiger moved off a little and made snuffling noises, then looked back at me like it were asking, *Come on, do you want to go with me?* I told Becky, *It's gonna take us home.* Course, she didn't want to be left alone and we followed the tiger into flat scrubby land chockablock with swamps and lakes. A freezing wind blew down from the snowy hills, so to keep warm we stayed on the move.

We were truly weary and with a terrible hunger when we arrived at a place between two trees hunchbacked by the wind. There were a hole in a bank surrounded by ferns and bracken, and the tiger went inside. I knew it must be its home. I peeked inside. It were real dim in there and then I seen the tiger staring back at me with eyes bright as burning coal and then another pair of eyes also poking into me soul. The cave were small and the floor covered in dried fern fronds. It smelt cosy and warm. I told Becky there were two tigers and I were going inside to be with them. She cried out that they would eat me. But I didn't think so cos I sensed they wouldn't eat me inside their home. I crawled in. The female tiger, the one we had been following, licked me arm. The other sniffed and snaffled me. I patted them. Me goodness I were fearless when I be a kid – I don't know if I could do that now. I felt like I were with two gentle dogs. I called out to Becky saying it were all right but she moaned and worried in fear. I peered out of the den and seen she were shivering and pale like death. I told her not to be stupid and join us. She were very stubborn and shaked her head again and again. *It's warm inside*, I said, and thumped me chest to prove they did not eat me. Her teeth started to chatter with fear and the cold. I could take no more of her stubbornness and I grabbed her arm and pulled her inside. She cried out, *No, no!* Which upset the tigers, so much they huddled up against the wall. With the four of us inside the den there were hardly much room. I been told a deadhouse next to a hotel were like this, cramped and small, so drunks could sleep away the booze, but this were an alive place with four creatures, two tigers and us two girls. Becky stopped crying and stayed near the opening. She could not look at the tigers. *They're not going to eat you*, I said. I hugged the bitch. *See, they are friendly. This is the mummy one*, I said, and I pointed to the other one. *That's the daddy one. They both have fur like me mother's coat.* I were now very knackered and I were very sleepy. I lay down next to the tigers and the mother one lay down with me. Becky were still suspicious and she crawled in a little bit more and sat up against a wall staring at the tigers, just waiting for them to try and eat her. Me? I went to sleep.

I am amazed I could do that. I could go to sleep real easy. Becky weren't an animal girl. Me? I loved animals and were never scared of them, except maybe a Tasmanian Devil and who wouldn't be afeared of a devil? So I had no trouble sleeping, though when I woke up I was tossed in me head for a short time cos I wondered where I were. Then I realised I were in the tigers' lair. But there were no tigers. It were dark in the cave and gloaming outside. I seen Becky curled up on the floor of ferns, deep asleep. I were 'bout to say, *Hello Becky* when suddenly, like she heard something awful in a dream, she wakes up, her eyes wide and alert. I heard a noise too and the opening to the den went dark. It were one of the tigers. It came into the cave, a step ahead of the sunlight that poured in again. Becky whimpered like a pup and crawled away from the creature. It had a dead bird in its mouth.

The tiger dropped the bird on me lap. It were bloody and its head chewed, its belly tore open. I knew it were a present. *Thank you*, I said, and I swear, I swear on me mother and father's heart, that it knew what I said cos it kind of nodded as if saying

Eat it and trotted outside. The bird felt warm when I touched it and I dipped me finger into its bloody chest and licked the blood off me finger. It tasted rich like molasses. Becky made disgusted noises. *It's not cooked*, she groaned. I told her I remember me father telling me stories 'bout how he ate snakes and cockroaches, so a bird were fine to eat. I were starving and the taste of blood made me feel even more hungry. I tried to pick at it with me fingers but I couldn't get any flesh so I bit at its chest til I got some flesh and then chewed it. It felt sort of cooked cos it were still warm. *Ugh! Ugh!* Becky kept on saying, but it were fine to taste though hard to chew. I could feel the blood dribbling down me chin and for some reason it made me happy – I could feel me tummy filling up a little and that felt good. I gave the bird to Becky, who knocked it away. I picked it up and wiped the dirt from it. I told Becky she had to eat, but she shaked her head something frightful. As I chewed up more of the bird, pulling out feathers from between me teeth, Becky called me a cannibal.

Aye, I am a cannibal, I grinned. Well, that were more than she could put up with and she skedaddled out of the cave on her hands and legs.

I ate some more and then crawled out of the den. Becky were sitting between the buttress roots of one of the two trees eating some grass and leaves. She were looking at her mother's cameo and she were murmuring to herself words I did not hear. I thought I would play a joke on her, you know, make her laugh, so I silently crawled up behind her then made snuffling noises like a tiger. She jumped in fright. I laughed and she slapped me across the face. It stanged like mad. *What was that for?* I cried. She snarled like an animal. *You sleep with them. You make noises like them!* All I could say were that I liked the tigers and they didn't hurt us. *You like them more than your mother and father?* she sneered, her words stanging me again. She jumped up like a Jack-in-the-box and said, *I'm going home.* She asked me if I were coming. I were still angry with her and shaked me head. She walked off in the direction of the setting sun, which I thought were the wrong way cos home were in the east. I knew that cos me father had teached me about the compass needle and where home were just in case I got lost. *You're going the wrong way, gink!* I called out. She began to get smaller and smaller. I were cold and lonely so I crawled back into the cave wondering what to do. I knew Becky were going the wrong way but I had no idea where I were either. I gave up worrying cos I were still hungry and I started to chew on the bird again. Then after a time, oh, I don't know how long, I heard a noise at the entrance of the cave. I thought it were the tigers but I seen it were Becky, her teeth chattering with the cold. Without a word, she crawled into the hole and sat against the wall, hugging herself, watching me eat the rest of the bird.

Me and Becky must have been dog-tired cos we slept through the night. Becky were so tired she did not notice that she were sleeping with the tigers and were cuddling up to them. We needed them; they were warm and our dresses were thin. In the morning I woke up first and seen her sleeping with the tigers. It were then, like I were whacked over me head, that I realised just how large the tigers were compared to us. Aye, I thought, they could eat us but they weren't going to. I seen the female tiger's belly and it had swollen teats that were leaking milk. I felt sad for her.

Becky woke when she heard me crawling outside. The tigers stirred and then, as if awful weary, stayed dozing when Becky followed me outside. It were a warm day and I drunk some water. I just lapped it up and Becky got annoyed with me saying I were drinking like the tigers – but it were quicker, I said back to her. She said, *No, we drink like this* and she cupped her hands and drank like from a mug, but I knew that licking it up were quicker and I didn't get water all over me dress.

We sat in the shade of the two trees and Becky sighed a lot. She were full of sadness and despair. *They aren't going to take us home, Hannah,* she said. *This is their home so why would they take us back to our home?* It made sense, but what could we do? I didn't know me way back to the Munro River and we had no way of finding our way back. *If we stay here, then someone will find us,* I said. But she were in a bitter mood and shook her head. *No, we are lost. We are gone forever,* she said real quiet, and cos her words were so certain I thought that she were telling the truth 'bout our plight and she were right. I heard her stomach rumble something fierce – I told her she should have eaten the bird with me. *Pooh,* she said and walked to a bush that had red berries on it and gobbled some. I were hungry but I lost me pangs when Becky started to vomit. Up they came, all the chewed berries, and she hugged her stomach and moaned and groaned in pain. I didn't know what to do and I were afeared she might die. The female tiger came out of the cave and sniffed Becky as she were curled up in pain between the buttress tree roots. Then the tiger looked at me with her glowing eyes and went back inside the den. I felt better cos it seemed to me that the tiger had sniffed the pain and decided Becky were going to be all right.

And she were right as rain after a couple of hours. We were outside talking 'bout what we should do for food when I felt something touch me arm. It were the female tiger nuzzling me. The male tiger came out of the den and walked down to the creek to drink, then the female followed it. They looked like wolves made out of gold when the setting sun stroked their fur. After drinking some water they both stared at us – as if they were asking a question. The bitch made a noise like it were a cross between a man's deep cough and a bark. Then the male tiger made a coughing bark at us. I thought this were funny, so I made a coughing bark in return. Then the two of them started to head off along the creek. I knew in me heart that the bark were kind of a signal, so I got up and joined them. *Where you going?* I heard Becky cry. I knew she were too scared to stay behind and I soon heard her hurrying up to join me.

We followed them along the creek, then across

some rocks and into the deep tara territory. I hadn't seen such weird green countryside, all tree ferns and moss and lichen on the rocks. The sun were washing itself across the trees and ferns – it were like the countryside had become more mysterious and beautiful. We got to a clearing where the tigers were waiting for us. I don't know why I did this, but the male tiger's tail was right next to me, so I grabbed it. It felt hard like a stick. The tiger spinned round and its jaws opened wider and wider like it were yawning so that its jaw were going to break til I thought it were going to swallow me, then suddenly, quick as a flash, it nipped me. I yelped and let go of the tail. I looked at the bite. It were a tiny thing, but Becky said, real nervous, *Did it hurt?* I told her the truth that, no, it didn't hurt much. The tiger looked at me straight in the eyes like it were giving me a real stern lesson and I knew never to touch its tail again. Cos I didn't want it to think I were upset or frightened, I opened up me jaws like it did. I tried to open them as wide as they could go, til I felt I were going to break me jaw. It must have been the right thing to do cos the tigers stepped away as if scared of me. Then they came forward. Becky did a big yawn and they backed off again. We laughed and the tigers moved right away from us. We were still laughing at them when they suddenly went all frozen. Their ears turned towards a sound they heard. The male tiger stood on his hind legs, like it were a human or a roo, so he could see over the high grass and ferns. Then without looking or coughing at each other they ran off. I felt this bolt of excitement flow through me and I found meself running after them, so did Becky. We got to a clearing and we seen a whole mob of wallabies in a right tizz. They were scattering everywhere. *Thump, thump, thump*, they went like the earth were a drum. The tigers picked on one and chased it down. The female rounded in front of the frightened thing, so that it spun round and hopped back towards us. Becky jumped away but I ran at it, trying to catch it. I were all excited, all hot and bothered, and were crying out, *Catch it, catch it!* I set off after the tigers who ran past me after the wallaby. It were mighty swift, I can tell you. I ran and fell and ran and fell after it. But it hopped faster than the tigers could run and soon it was gone, just a dot hopping away through the giant tree ferns. I fell down exhausted and heard meself, like I were an animal, screaming to the sky in disappointment. I dearly wanted to catch that wallaby for I were hungry, very hungry. Becky came up to me as I were lying on the ground and I took out me gall on her. *Why didn't you help us*, I cried. And she looked down at me with a face full of shock and surprise and then horror. *You're becoming one of them!* she spitted on me and walked off.

The tigers didn't find anything to kill that night so Becky and I ate pinkberries. I gave some to the tigers, who must have been very hungry because they ate them too. On the way back to the den or is it lair – I get mixed up – I said to Becky that we should give the tigers names. She were in a right sulky mood and said she didn't care, so I named the male tiger Dave and the female Corinna.

Now where did I get those names? Well, I think Dave came from me uncle Dave and Corinna from me aunt. He were thin as a stick and she were big like Sam. They came to visit us once before they went to South Africa to search for gold. He were a funny man and she were strange cos she had a moustache. A real moustache like she had a black caterpillar on her top lip. Me mother said to stop staring but I were a kid – who wouldn't stop looking at it? It were like when I saw a pure white wombat, what's that called? An albino. I couldn't stop staring at the moustache cos it were so different. So I guess that's where the names came from.

When we got back to the den I seen Becky sitting outside peering into the night at the distant hills all pale with moonlight and I asked her what she were looking for and she said her father. She said he'd be searching for us through every nook and cranny of Tasmania. I said, *That's blather*, it would be me father doing that, and she snarled like some animal,

You are a gink, Hannah. Those tigers are making you stupid like them. I hit her and went inside the den to sleep with the tigers cos dawn were coming up and I heard her yell after me, *They're dead.* It was then she told me, in a rush of hatred, that she had seen me drowned mother stuck in a tree – like she were tied to a mast – floating down the Munro to the sea. I said she were lying, but she said she weren't and that in all possibility of fate me father were drowned too and we now had to depend on her father, her father who loved her and would search for her for all time.

I were very cut up about what she told me and I put me hands over me ears and I sang a song real loud as she told me again and again what had happened to me mother and father. I weeped long and hard and went inside the den abusing her something bad. The tigers were scared of me loud singing and me tears. I plopped down on the fronds and were in misery. Corinna curled herself next to me and I found meself sucking her nipples, like it were the most natural thing in the world. I filled meself up to

49

brimful with her warm milk and it made me less sad and less feeling misery for meself. And I remember that as I fell asleep – the memory is still as sharp today – I felt myself to be an orphan now and alone. I did not like Becky for telling me what she seen, but deep down I knew she were telling the truth. That were a heavy burden for a girl me age.

Becky may have been picking on me, like a real gink, but she snuggled up with the tigers too, cos they were cosy to sleep with. We sleeped through the day and woke up near dusk and all our bellies were grumbling something terrible. The sun were warm outside and we followed the tigers through the bush hoping that they'd get some food. We were starving. 'Bout half an hour into our hunt the tigers went all still and their noses sniffed the breeze. They made a snuffling noise to each other and I knew that they had smelled prey. And I have to say me heart leaped up with joy, cos I were so hungry. The tigers ran through the bush into open country and there were before us a pack of wallabies contentedly eating grass. When they seen the tigers, and us behind them, they scattered in all directions; a willy-willy of fright. The tigers set after a small wallaby which hopped for its life. Dave circled in front of it, while Corinna chased behind it. Then Corinna stopped, turned and did a coughing bark back at us. I knew what that meant and, you know what, so did Becky, cos I seen her eyes light up too.

I raced to the other side, just in case the wallaby circled back round Corinna and as I am running I am so excited that I run into a damn tree and I bounce off – a real whack to me forehead and I fall to the ground. I heard Becky, all tizzy, laugh like I were a clown at a circus. I were a bit confused cos the tree hit me so hard. Becky ran past me, offering no hand to help, shouting at me, *Come on, gink! Here! Round it up!* So I jumped up and seen the wallaby turning round cos Dave had headed it off. I seen out of the corner of me eye the bitch tiger coughing at us, knowing we were in the hunt too. It were like she were giving orders and both Becky and I knew

51

which way to go to cut off the wallaby's escape. And, you know, both Becky and I were coughing barking too in all the excitement. Trying to escape from the tigers the wallaby found itself hopping towards me and Becky and we ran towards it, spaced a yard apart so it couldn't squeeze between us. It seen us, done a sort of a backflip and hopped back towards Dave, who jumped on the wallaby. His jaws were open so wide I thought they would break and he gripped it round the head. I heard, oh, maybe from a distance of thirty yards, the crunch of tiger teeth into the wallaby skull and I felt not disgust but joy. We all caught it! Holy Moses, oh me, oh me heart is going ten to the dozen just thinking about it, remembering that first time.

It were stone dead and Becky and me looked at each other, feeling we were like true hunters. We were panting as much as the tigers but I could see in Becky's eyes and in the tigers' eyes that we were all over the moon. Becky flopped onto the ground even more knackered than me or the tigers cos she hadn't had food or milk for some time. But she were happy and she lied on her back and stared up at me, saying, *We did it.* And indeed we did and I were proud too. I were hungry and moved to the dead wallaby but Dave opened his mouth with a real big yawn of threat so I jumped back. He gulped down the brain and ate bits of the heart and guts and then left the rest of the carcass for us. I jumped in to take me meal but Corinna nipped me on the back of me leg – I knew the nip meant *Wait your turn!* But before the tiger could eat her fill Becky suddenly threw herself on the wallaby. The bitch bit her too. Becky yelped and ran back a few yards to rub the teeth marks on her leg but then she did a thing I didn't think were in her. She began to crawl towards the wallaby, inch by inch, knowing the female tiger were sneaking glances at her as she ate but Becky didn't care. The tiger nipped her again. Becky did not yelp this time but stood her ground. The male tiger, he did nothing but watch what was happening with a sort of curious expression as if interested in how the duel would turn out. Then Becky jumped up, pushed the bitch out of the way and buried her face in the wallaby's bloody insides and, like she were a devil, she tore at it with teeth and fingers. She ate in a fury of hunger and growled when the bitch got close. I were amazed. I had never seen this part of Becky before. She were always a tame girl. I never seen her act like that; it were with such wildness. I were bug-eyed. She were braver than me too.

Becky stuffed herself. I tried to join her but she growled at me, warning me away. When she packed full her belly she sat in the grass, her mouth and face shiny red with blood. The female tiger then took her turn and I waited til last and I ate what were left. I were so hungry I didn't care what I ate, so I gutsed meself. When I were stomach-packed I sat in the grass feeling woozy with food. Becky and I didn't care we ate raw meat. Just goes to show you what hunger can do to a human. I watched Becky try and wipe her face free of blood with large dock leaves. She looked funny with a wet red face. I laughed and she did too. I were happy, as were the tigers who licked their chops free of blood. I realised that I had seen something of Becky that were new to me – she were really stubborn if she wanted something. She were brave, she were stubborn, she were smart, she were tough. A devil came out of the long grass walking that funny way like it were a rocking horse. It snorted and growled at us but we didn't care. Then it gnawed and teared its way into the carcass til it had its full too.

That night, well, it were really a couple of hours before dawn, when we got back to the den we sat outside in the warm moonlight . . . all four of us. We were full as googs. Becky were thoughtful and touched her mother's cameo a lot like she were thinking of home. I were yawning and thinking of going to bed when she noticed something. *Hey, where's your shoes?* I forgot I had taken them off during the hunt. *They hurt*, I said. Becky looked at her own shoes and I knew she were thinking that she might take hers off, but she didn't. I think she were afeared she would become like an animal and stop being a human. She heard an owl hoot. *We have a barn owl at home*, she said, and sounded very lonely. The female tiger got up, and as she were heading inside the cave, she rubbed herself against me, sniffed me face and licked me hand. She were saying in her own lingo, *We are all in this together.*

It sounds foolish, but when you are so close to some creature like a tiger you get to really know them and that's what Corinna were saying to me – *We are a pack.* I followed her inside, leaving Becky out in the night gazing face full of sadness at the moon, the owl, the cameo, like she were possessed by thoughts of home. I would have thought of home but I were dead beat and besides – did I have a home to go back to? Me mother were dead – that much was certain cos Becky told me. But what about me father? Maybe he were out with Mr Carsons searching for us. Becky prayed for this. Sometimes I'd see her by herself kneeling in the ferns, her hands pressed together, mumbling her prayers and looking at the sky as if her father were going to come down like manna from heaven. She were a bit older than me in age but she were much more older than me in many other ways, so she had this burden or sense of responsibility and I were the biggest burden of them all, she said to me more than once. She feared I were becoming an animal but I knew that without the tigers there were no food for us, no warm bodies to sleep with, us four snuggled like a bundle of fleshy yarn in each other's embrace.

The tigers stopped being animals to me. They were Corinna and Dave. She were a bit smaller than him and she had black hairs sprinkled on her white upper lip. Dave's were just white. He liked us but kept his distance cos he had a lot of things on his mind, like protecting us, keeping an eye open for prey or enemies like bounty hunters. Corinna showed she liked us by licking us and curling up with us whenever we slept. Though I have to say, if she didn't like something you did, she'd nip you to let you know. Their eyes were full black and they had a sort of inner glow so that at dusk they shone green and sometimes red. They liked to bask in the sun but tried to avoid looking into harsh light if possible. It were something that I were learning. I might be studying them, but they studied us as well. When they looked deep at you, you knew they were peering right into your soul and they knew if you were lying or not. You couldn't pretend to them that you were happy when you were not. They knew when we were down in the dumps and would nuzzle and comfort us.

One time I laughed and said to Becky, *Things are topsy-turvy, we sleep during the day and we be awake all night.* She didn't find it funny cos she knew that meant the tigers had changed us and she didn't like that one bit.

There wasn't a time when I realised I were becoming like a tiger, I guess it just happened, like it were natural. But when I think back there were signs that I had changed, and Becky too. Our sight got better at night. Once nighttime were as thick as mud to me, but now it were like clear water. And me hearing – I could sit in silence and hear so many things that I did not hear before: the movement of fern leaves, like the bristles of a brush being stroked, when a quoll were passing (the black ones with white spots like a starry night coming to life) or the sharp cry of pain in a tree when a quoll knocked a sleeping bird off a branch and catched it in mid-air; the squeal of a mouse being taken by an owl whose wings sounded like the creaking of a ship; the whisper of dead leaves as an adder slid over them; the coughing of a distant tiger, like a pipe-smoker clearing his throat of spew; a barking snake; a possum munching on fruit; the devils yowling and snarling like something from hell when they were fighting over a dead animal. And the smells – soon I could tell the difference between the dung of all sorts of animals. Even the most stinky shit were interesting cos it were mixed up with the smell of seeds, animal flesh and fruit. There were many sorts of piss and it told you all sorts of things – what sort of animal, how old, how pregnant, how sick. I could sniff shit and know what sort of animal it were, and when I got really good I could tell how fresh it were. We learned to be downwind so our prey couldn't smell us. And I learned something else: Corinna stopped feeding me her milk when her teats dried up and I realised why she had taken a liking to us. Her pups had died or more likely been killed by a bounty hunter. She thought we were babies so that's why she took us in. Then I said to Becky that I hated that tiger man who stayed with me and me parents cos he murdered tiger pups.

It were not only bounty hunters who killed them as I found out one late afternoon when we were walking through the bush. It started to drizzle so we took shelter under an over-hanging rock that looked like some sort of sandy frozen wave. I were glancing up at the roof when I seen some paintings on it. *They must have been done by the blackfellas when*

they were kings of Tasmania, said Becky. There were four drawings of what looked like dogs but because they had stripes on them we knew were tigers.

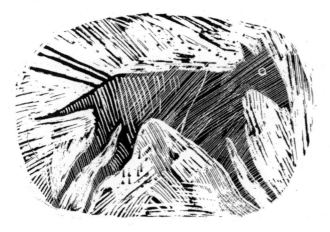

One had three spears sticking out of its flanks. We both went *Oh* at the same time, cos it made us sad to see how even blackfellas killed tigers. I remember us running our hands over the picture of the speared tiger, like we were trying to help it or save it cos there beside us was our saviours – Dave and Corinna. I felt terrible. For days I dreamed about our two tigers being speared by blackfellas and it were more night-mare, much more nightmare, than dream. Becky told me she had those nightmares too. See, we were family. We did not think that at the time, but when I look back, I know we were family and that's the truth of it.

It were now summer, bright and hot, filled with so much lightning that trees burst into flames and burned for days. I loved going out hunting during these warm nights. We slept in the den of a day, keeping away from the terrible heat and the flies, millions and millions of them, that swarmed over us, filling our eyes and ears with their squirming, tickling bodies. And at night the snakes were gone.

We and the tigers hated snakes. Sometimes at night we might come upon one of those damn snakes curled up on a warm log, its belly big with some small animal it had got, and the four of us made a wide circle round it, even though it weren't interested in us.

One night when the full moon were glaring bright, we went hunting. We ended up passing through a forest of ferns taller than us when I seen a pair of bright burning eyes. It were a devil, and instead of being afeared I were cocky and I jumped at it, snarling and hissing like they do, and it took fright and skedaddled. Becky just shook her head, as if to say *You are a right Tom Fool, Hannah*, but I didn't care cos I knew the tigers liked me courage. We drank water from the creek not far from the ferny forest and again Becky sneered at me for lapping up the water like the tigers but it were quick and water didn't drip through me hands like it did to her.

We four sat listening to the night sounds, hearing every little thing and Becky and me seeing into the darkness like we were born with sharp eyes. As we waited to hear the sounds of some animal we might kill come to drink at the creek, Becky looked up at the tree above us and climbed up it like a monkey. She made it look easy. When I asked what she were doing she said she had seen some fruit. She started throwing down berries the size of small apples. I tasted one. It were sour and I wondered if the fruit were poisonous but she said she had a tree like this one at home and it were safe to eat. She chucked down lots of fruit and then jumped down to join us. It was then that I were glad I had hands, cos it were easier to eat holding the fruit than for the tigers who only had their mouths. So I hand-fed them and you know what? Becky started to do it too. We could do things for them, and they could do things for us we couldn't do.

Becky seemed more happy than I ever seen her since

that dreadful day of the picnic. She were rocking back and forth, humming and eating the fruit. I asked her if she were happy and she said she were. I asked the tigers if they were happy. Becky called me stupid. *They can't talk, Hannah.* I told her that might be true, but they could understand me. It were then that Becky suddenly stood up, an action that caused me to jump and the tigers to go alert as if something dangerous were round us. I asked her what were the matter? She didn't say anything but were frantic as she searched round the base of the tree in the long grass, til she found what she were looking for and showed me. It were her mother's cameo shining in the moonlight. I thought it were funny she was worried about losing it, but she said it belonged to her mother and it were the only thing of hers she had. *That's all I got,* she moaned. *I got nothing of me father's and only this to remind me of me dead mother.* I hated her misery talk so I climbed up the tree and threw some more fruit to the tigers. From the tree branch I were standing on I looked down and I seen Becky sitting on the grass staring at the cameo, like it belonged to a different life, to a part of her which were a long time ago and she were trying to remember. I dropped a fruit on her head. She yelled, *Ouch!* and looked up at me. Instead of being angry she were deeply sad. *We will never go home*, she said. It struck me to the core of me heart to hear her say that. Aye, she were right. We would never go home. I stood on the tree branch and looked out towards the moon-kissed mountains. *One day we'll get home*, I said. She just shook her head.

Perhaps it were good that Becky thought that, cos she became closer and more loving to the tigers. She understood that it were the four of us against Nature and only by being close would we survive. She never criticised me being close to Dave and Corinna again. After a night hunting and gorging on prey, me and the tigers would go back and sleep. Becky liked to stay outside the den watching dawn come up and she'd talk to herself, singing rhymes, reciting the colours of the rainbow using a chant a teacher had given her ('Richard of York Gave Battle in Vain'), arithmetic tables and fairytales her father had read to her. She didn't want to forget. Me? I thought it were stupid to try and remember like Becky did. I didn't see any use for it. Me English started to shrivel up, like an old dry skin a snake gets rid of. It just lies there in the grass rotting away and then vanishes with the wind. I took to talking in grunts, coughs and hoarse barks like the tigers. This annoyed Becky no end. But it were simple – the tigers understood me. Becky warned I were making a mistake. *You will forget your language. You will forget your parents. You are becoming an animal,* she'd say. Why argue with her? She were right on every level.

One autumn evening when the air were full of chill we went out hunting. There were less and less animals 'bout and the birds were flying north. It were weeks since we were full up to dolly's wax. The tigers must have known what autumn meant cos they didn't bother to sniff out prey and one evening set off at a steady pace in the opposite direction of our usual hunting grounds. I knew what that meant. They were planning on a long walk. We headed off through tara fern country and once we had left the green world we moved through a forest of blue and silver gums, taking a wide berth round giant fields of barking brilla that we knew were squirming with tiger snakes, and headed down the slopes.

Becky and I wondered where we were going, but the tigers had no way of explaining to us so we could only follow. Becky were thinking out loud at one point, becoming excited that they might be taking us home. I didn't think so, but they had a purpose in mind cos they seemed to be dead certain where they were going. The good thing were that as we went further downhill the warmer it became. It had been hard to keep warm at times cos I had little of me dress left. It were really just a piece of ripped material that hanged on me like a useless kerchief, and Becky's, although she was always trying to look after it, were torn too and she used the cameo to pin together two pieces at the top of her dress. She didn't want anyone to see her chest. *Who cares? Who's gonna see your tits out here?* I'd say, which really made her cranky. She thought I were right grubby but I didn't care. I were wearing bits of me dress but I had thrown away me underclothes. It were easier to piss and shit without them. Becky still washed hers in the creek and wouldn't be seen without them.

Just after dawn the tigers stopped. They sniffed the air. We sniffed the air too. There were the smell of smoke. Becky burst into a grin as wide as a tiger's yawn. I always remembered what she said then, in an excited voice, her eyes sparkling: *A house! That's someone's fire!* Without waiting for us, she ran off through the brush and up a slope where she stopped and stared at something I could not see. I raced to join her and there through a mist of trees were a wooden shack with smoke puffing out of the tin chimney. There were someone there! Me heart beat so loud I thought I were going deaf. We were looking at the cottage when I seen a figure, a man with a wild ginger beard, step off the back verandah and walk towards his horse tied to a tree. *It's a man,* she said, excited and twitching as if stanged by jack jumpers. She were about to yell out to the man when I slapped her arm.

I recognised him; it were that terrible tiger man who sometimes stayed with me parents. Then I seen he were holding something that made me want to piss meself. I squeezed Becky's arm real hard. She spun round wanting to hit me. I pointed to a huge carving knife he had in his hand.

So what! she replied, thumping me back. I were aware of a padding sound behind us and seen the two tigers had joined us. They too were watching this fella as it began to drizzle. There were something 'bout the way he held the knife that scared me. I thought he were going to kill the horse but he threw the knife into the ground and untied a bundle that were strapped to its back. I heard Becky gasp. It were a dead tiger. Then before we had time to think what this meant, he pulled the knife out of the earth and made a deep cut along the tiger's belly. He were good at what he were doing. In next to no time he had skinned that tiger, ripping its skin off in one tremendous yank. He carried the skin to a lean-to round the side of the shack then went back inside as it began to pour down something shocking.

The horse sniffed the shiny skinned body of the tiger and went back to eating grass. Both Becky and I looked at our tigers and hoped that they didn't know what were happening, but they knew. Their noses were working over-time cos they smelt raw flesh and blood. Their tails were rigid with fright. *Come on*, said Becky, grabbing me, *let's go to him.*

I shook me head, I didn't like that man. I didn't like anyone who killed tigers. Becky didn't wait for me answer and crept closer. I followed. The horse looked up when it seen us and made a snuffling noise. Becky stared at the dead tiger. It looked like something out of a nightmare. Its veins and pink bloody flesh were awful to see and it seemed so helpless, so naked as the rain fell on it, causing the blood to weep down its sides into the earth.

I thought Becky were going to run inside the house, but she were heading towards the lean-to. There were no door and by the time I had reached her she were stiff as a statue, standing in the doorway gobsmacked. I peered inside. O my, O my, me heart and brain were filled with shock and the most awful pain. I had to suck in me breaths so as to not cry or faint. The lean-to were filled with tiger skins all nailed to the walls or hanging from the beams – all in different stages of curing, so it stank like a swamp filled with rotting animals. I think I lost most of me language there. I mean, where are the words to explain what I seen? There must have been twenty or so skins, male and female, big and small. It were like a slaughterhouse. I felt sick to me stomach and coughed up a purple vomit of berries. I felt like I were nailed to the earth. I couldn't move. Becky grabbed me and put her fingers to her lips, telling me to be quiet. I followed her from the lean-to round to the front of the house. The tigers had backed away and were staring at us from the bush. Their eyes were full of fear and trembling for us and for them. I wanted to join them but Becky were curious 'bout something and she grabbed me by the hand and led me to the shack.

We creeped onto the front verandah and looked in through a grubby window. There were the murderer sitting and watching his billy boil in the fireplace. He had taken off his wet clothes and were drying them in front of the fire. He himself were naked as the day he were born, as if he too had been skinned. Above the fireplace were a huge tiger skin nailed to the wall. I could stand no more and found meself walking down the side of the house back to the tigers. Becky stopped me, asking where I were going. It seemed right obvious to me. I were going back to the tigers. *No, we ask him to take us back home*, whispered Becky. *He won't kill us.* I shrugged her off. I couldn't think straight. All I knew was that our tigers, who were still waiting for us at the top of the slope, had to be warned to run, to run as far as possible away from this goddamn awful place. *He's just a bounty hunter*, she said. I told her I knew the tiger man with the ginger hair. He had stayed with me parents and me. I had never liked him. He smelt like shit and death. I were afeared this fella would kill us and skin us too, that's how close I were to the tigers. *All right*, she said. *You go with Dave and Corinna. Me, I'm going to ask for his help in getting home.* I said nothing and walked back to the tigers. Becky disappeared round the front of the house. I ran me hands over the tigers' backs. Their hair were bristling with terror. Just the thought of seeing their skins on the wall above the fireplace were enough

74

for me to think to flee and flee and flee til I dropped dead of exhaustion.

Then, when I thought Becky were gone for good, I seen her tearing down the side of the house towards us, shouting, *Run! Run!* The man appeared round the side of the house brandishing a shotgun. The strange thing were that he were still naked, except for boots. Becky cut across the back yard, jumping over the skinned corpse of the tiger and scaring the horse so that it reared up on its back legs, and ran towards us. The man were calling out, *Come back!* But we were shit-scared – the four of us – and raced off, heading down the slope, into the mess of trees and through the button grass. I expected to hear shots, but there were none, only faint calls for us to come back. We were full of panic and we ran til we could run no more. When we stopped the tigers' tongues were hanging out and ours were too cos we were panting so hard.

The rain were growing thick and we looked for some shelter and found an overhanging rock pale green with lichen. I asked Becky if she had talked to the tiger man. *I were going to go inside*, she said, *when I seen something.* I asked her what she seen but she closed her mouth real firm and shooked her head til she got sick of me questions, and suddenly snapped at me, *He were doing stuff to himself that were rude.* I had no idea what she were talking 'bout and even though I pestered her for days, she wouldn't tell me. Then it didn't matter any more. But I were glad we didn't ask him for help. I couldn't have asked anybody for help who did what men like him did to tigers. Tiger men are the spawn of Lucifer. I think Becky were glad too. She had seen things she didn't want to see again.

We slept til evening and set off downhill, finding some shrivelled heartberries that had fallen on the ground. One time we came upon some rusted-out boilers. It were the ruins of a piners' camp and the boilers were where the men distilled the Huon pine oil. We were walking on a gum tree that had fallen across a creek when I slipped on the mossy trunk and fell into the water. It took me some time to reach the bank and I were a right sight. Me body were one squirming mass of shiny black leeches, on me legs, arse, arms and a couple sucking at me nose. It took me and Becky some time to remove them all. Oh, I shiver even now at the thought of those dreadful creatures sucking me blood.

We travelled for a few more days – forget how many – til one late afternoon I stood on a hill and seen the horizon flat as a pancake. It were the distant sea. Then I knew: it were the coast we had been making for. And I knew it were what Dave and Corinna had been aiming for all along. The way the tigers moved through the countryside to the sea was real dead certain. They were used to doing this.

The day before we reached the sea the four of us dozed in a small cave that could barely fit us all in. Becky couldn't sleep and woke me up and said to me in a voice full of real purpose. *That man who*

killed all those tigers were a bad man and he would have killed us. We will find a good man somewhere round here and he'll take us home. I knew she were saying it for me own good but she were also saying it for hers, to try and calm down her dread. We had come close to getting home and next time, she were saying in that bent way of hers, we would find a man who would rescue us. But really, I didn't think much of being saved. I were a kid, a child, and children get used to a lot of things and I were now used to this way of life, unlike Becky. Sure, I missed me father and me mother but cos I reckoned they were dead it were becoming easy for me to get used to this new world and it were becoming second nature to me. That evening round dusk we reached the sea.

It were calm and flat like a verandah floor. We were starving and I were disappointed. What were there to eat? Why had Dave and Corinna come this far? The tigers went off towards some rocks and after Becky and I couldn't find food, we joined them. They were ripping mussels off the rocks and crunching them up as they ate them. Becky and I couldn't do that, so we broke the mussels off their perch and after smashing the shells open ate the flesh. Oh, we ate so many. I can still taste their soft, salty meat. It were so different from what we had been eating. Even though I remembered eating mussels me father had brought back from Hobart, these were different, they were real fresh, plump, really fatty plump, and we laughed and laughed as Becky and me popped mussels down each other's throats and down the throats of the tigers, who liked us doing it cos the meat didn't have any shell bits. Once I cut me ankle on a mussel shell but I didn't care. Corinna licked me blood til the wound closed and I s'pose because of the sea water it didn't become infected.

The tigers didn't head back from the beach near dawn, instead they waited near the sand dunes facing the sun, their eyes and bodies alert. Then as the sun came up, washing the sea in light so it shone brightly, black dots appeared and disappeared in the golden water. I heard the tigers' throats rumble and their noses sniff hard. Their bodies trembled with excitement as the dots swam closer. Then the dark blobs emerged from the sea, flopping and scrambling up on the beach. They were seals and about the size of me and Becky. I seen the tigers' fur bristle and their tails go stiff. Then before I knew what was happening they were rushing across the dunes down to the wet sand where the seals were making their way to the rocks. Dave jumped at the throat of one and ripped it open. Corinna leaped on a smaller one and did the same. The seals were hollering and squealing. Dave looked back at us with his eyes burning bright with the scent of blood. He were calling us. I ran down to join them. I heard Becky calling me back, but I didn't care. I were excited by the smell of blood too. When I reached the tigers they were putting their snouts down the throats of the seals and ripping out their tongues which they chewed up in a blink of an eye and then they were off to kill more. I didn't know what to do. I had never eaten seal before. I didn't fancy the tongue but then I knew the tigers wouldn't let me have any tongues cos they were in a right frenzy ripping them out of every seal they killed. Becky came up to me trembling at the slaughter and the agonised groans of the seals and their squealing, squeaking pain. *This is terrible. This is terrible*, she kept on saying. It turned me guts a bit, especially the cries of the seals, but mostly I were not that upset about it. I knew I had to eat.

God knows where me sense of survival came from. Maybe it's natural cos humans are just animals too. But I went over to the rocks which were slippery with blood and got meself a mussel shell, which I knew would be as sharp as a knife. I used it to slit open a seal's belly. Inside were hearts and lungs and stomach. I licked some of the blood and then cut off a hunk of the black skin which had pink flesh sticking to it. The outer skin were tough and tasteless but the inner lining were fresh and pink and was like chewing gristle. Even though it didn't seem to taste like anything special – in fact, it were a bland taste – it had this real odd effect, as if me skin were suddenly alive. The prickly feeling started in me upper lip near me nostrils and then headed up both sides of me nose and met in the middle of me brow where people think a third eye is and *Bang!* there were this explosion of high spirits in me. I were grinning like a fool. I looked round me. Becky's pained expression seemed funny, the tigers ripping out the tongues of the seals seemed wonderful and the sea were made from gold.

Some men say that when they drink whiskey there is a moment when they feel the happiest they have ever felt, when they feel like they can move mountains, chop down a tree with their bare hands or wrestle a man to death. Well, that's how I felt.

What were ever in that shiny pink gristle surged through me in waves of ecstasy. Becky asked if anything were the matter. I think I told her to try some of the pink flesh. I were cutting great chunks of it away from the black outer skin and chewing and chewing and chewing til me forehead were full of joy. Becky ate some and she became like me. She were ecstatic too. She danced along the wet sand. I danced with her and ran with the tigers who were jumping with high spirits too cos of something maybe similar in the seal tongues, and we ran and played til way into the afternoon. I had never had so much aliveness in me. Becky yafflered and yafflered at me, but the tigers and me paid no attention to her. We didn't want to talk. When the sun were on top of our heads we found some shelter behind the sand dunes and we slept snuggled up to each other. I could feel Becky's heart, Dave's and Corinna's racing hearts, as I put me head against their chests and fell asleep.

Seal gristle and tongues became our one and

only food, and that food were the cause of so much happiness. We were there for some days, I don't know how many cos I lost track of time. The seals stopped coming ashore and we could only kill the stragglers who had lost themselves from the main pod. One evening after the four of us had feasted on one scrawny thing, Dave spinned round as if he heard a noise but then I saw his nose were working overtime and I realised he smelt something powerful in the sea. He jumped from the rocks into the water and started to swim towards a dark object about the size of a cabbage. But he couldn't reach it and had to turn back. He and Corinna stood on the rocks staring at this thing bouncing on the incoming waves, their bodies straining towards it, as if they thought their necks could grow long enough for them to grasp it. Becky seen their hunger for it so she jumped off the rocks into the water. She started to walk through the waves towards it. She were taller than me, but the water rose up to her waist, then chest and neck and still she went forward. I were out of me skin with worry cos sometimes the waves completely swamped her and she vanished beneath them, frightening me to the core of me heart. Then when I thought she would surely drown and I were pissing meself with fright I seen her hand reach out of the boiling white foam and grab the thing. She allowed the waves to carry her back on shore. We three ran from the rocks to the wet sand where she lay coughing and spluttering but still holding it.

It were a greyish colour, with sharp bits of bone and shells sticking out of it. The tigers sniffed it. The smell made their tails go stiff with rapture. They nibbled at it. I knew I had to wait me turn but I couldn't wait. I grabbed it for meself. The tigers yawned at me and their eyes burned darkness into me, but I knew what I held in me hands – ambergris. It smelt of rotten stink and perfume. I told Becky what it were. She asked what it were for. I told her and said that if Dave and Corinna could eat it, then we could too. I gave it back to the tigers who were coughing threats at me. After they had chewed a mouthful the tigers' eyes went glassy and their legs gave up under them. They wobbled off to the dunes where they lied down and watched the stars. I ate a mouthful and felt me blood become perfume. I couldn't eat any more. It were richer than plum pudding. It were more powerful than seal gristle. I felt me legs turn soft, as if me bones had melted. I crawled to the dunes to join the tigers. Becky picked up the ambergris where I dropped it and carried it to the dunes where she ate a mouthful. Halfway through chewing it, she sighed, her eyes rolled back in her head, her expression were ecstatic and she fell down beside us real slow like she were in a dream, and when she landed next to me she sent up a puff of fine sand like dust in a room bright with sunlight.

We lied in the dunes like pieces of jelly. The next few days that's all we did. We ate ambergris til there were none left, except for the sharp bony things that were stuck in it. Sometimes I thought I were filled with honey. Other times I felt me body were a fish. I dreamt with me eyes open about whales. I dreamt with me eyes open about me father living inside a whale and it made me happy. Becky and I hardly said a word to each other. We were beyond words. When we moved round we did it on all fours, like we had become tigers too. I took off me dress and threw it away. I had no use for that, no use for words. Becky and me were in a heaven made of clouds of perfume. The tigers too. We all had the same expressions of bliss and happiness and we all had eyes that were glassy. We were full as a goog with joy.

Once the ambergris were finished, we slept for a couple of days and nights. I were now naked as the day I came into the world and Becky seeing me so carefree took off her dress and threw it away. It were a big thing for her to do but the dress were ragged and torn. She still wore her underclothes and put the cameo inside them so she wouldn't lose it. One late afternoon when we were back to our real selves, and it were time to go, we set off the way we had come, avoiding the tiger man, and heading back to the den. It became colder on our journey home, but the lair were warm, especially after we followed the example of the tigers, who ripped off fern fronds and put them on the floor. Becky took off her filthy underclothes and wrapped the cameo in them and put it in the corner of the den cos it were precious to her. I think in becoming naked it made her even more determined not to lose her language and she'd sing, tell stories from the Bible or recite poems, not caring if we listened or not. The deepest part of her were fighting real hard not to become an animal.

Winter is cruel. It's like having your bare bum whipped with a switch every day. It's a constant sting, especially in your stomach. We were in ferny country so there were still animals 'bout, but not as many. Cos we wore no clothes we covered ourselves with mud from the creek. The wind didn't cut us half as bad then. When snow fell we just stayed in our lair, snuggled up, snoozing all the time. Sometimes when we were really desperate for food we'd find a dead devil, but the flesh were rank and some of it would not stay down in our throat and it would come up again, but it were warm by then so we chewed it again and it were easier to swallow warm gunk. We went after wombat babies cos the mother and father were away hunting for their food. The tigers digged out the opening then Becky and I would attack the hole with sticks, digging deeper and deeper til we found the wombat pups. They were good nights. But in the real dark cold part of winter there were no food.

One evening as we looked out on the deep snow and shivered we knew it would be bad hunting. All our usual prey were in their burrows or dens. The world outside were empty of life. Our stomachs were full-bore empty too. Becky said she had an idea. So the three of us followed her through the ferny country, through the gum tree forest and into the scrub. We were still walking hours later when the sick sun came up.

We stopped on top of a hill and me heart started to beat like it were an animal trying to escape from me rib-cage. This were where the evil tiger man lived. The tigers were frightened too; I could see by their stiff tails. I were clutching Becky's muddy arm and saying, *No, no, no*. I didn't want to give meself up to the man cos he skinned the tigers. She looked at me hard – oh dear, I remember that look so well, it were branded on me brain. It said I were stupid and silly and weak. She dragged me up to the top of the slope. The horse were still there, its blanket covered in snow – it looked white like a unicorn in me picture book. There were no smoke coming from the chimney so the fella might have been sleeping or away hunting tigers, I didn't know. *There*, said Becky pointing to a dozen sheep dozing under a gum tree. I knew right then, like being whacked over the head with a piece of ironwood, that the sheep were our food. So did the tigers. There were no words said. We all knew we had to do this quickly and quietly. And we knew our part in the hunt.

The tigers ran in a wide arc so they could be behind the sheep while Becky and I herded them. We knew they would turn tail and run. Once we seen the tigers had cut off the sheep's escape route we ran straight at them. It were only later that I realised I were on all fours. It seemed more natural. We were so good at hunting, and so silent, that we were practically on the sheep before they realised. They tried to flee, but they went straight into the jaws of Dave and Corinna, who ripped the throats of two of the sheep while the others escaped. The horse were afeared and tried to get away but it were tied to a tree. We stood there, the dead sheep at our feet, panting and listening hard to any movement inside the shack. But there were none. I wanted to eat the sheep then and there and so did the tigers, but Becky said no. She were very quiet and forceful. She grabbed a sheep by the legs and told me to do the same. We dragged those two creatures from the back yard up the slope and boy it were hard yakka, let me tell you. It were easier going down the slope into a hiding place deep in a forest of peppermint gums, where we ate with a fury only the truly hungry could understand. Then Becky and me took turns carrying the remains of the sheep back to the den.

We became full of life and Becky and I didn't feel the cold quite as bad. The tigers started the habit of going off by themselves, not wanting us to come. It were strange behaviour and I couldn't figure out what they were doing. Then one day, as the sun were setting, Becky were outside when she called to me. I crawled out of the lair and seen what she were seeing. Dave were mounting Corinna in a clearing covered with snow. I had seen this sort of thing with me pigs. I knew they were making babies and so did Becky. I were troubled. Not by what they were doing, but what it meant for Becky and me.

Near the end of winter we ran out of food again so we went back to the bounty hunter's place. We killed two more sheep. After we gorged ourselves til late morning in our hideaway in the forest of gum trees, Becky got it in her head to go back to the shack. There were no smoke coming from the chimney, there were no horse and there were no sign of the tiger man. I followed her, trembling a little cos I was worried he would spot us, but she had purpose on her mind.

We snuck round to the front of the shack and peered into the window. The house seemed empty. We pushed open the front door and stood there in the doorway. Me fear was so bad that I felt meself leaking, a warm trickle running down the inside of me legs. Becky stood there for a time listening, and let me tell you, our hearing were extra good now. I could hear the footsteps of a dunnart on dead leaves a hundred yards away, and know that a low growl were a wombat and a solitary crunch sound were a quoll crushing a rabbit's skull with a bite to the back of the neck. And our eyes, our eyes could see way deep into the darkness and recognise the shape of a pademelon or pygmy possum hiding in a night tree. Becky heard nothing. She looked at me, I heard nothing too, so we stepped inside.

It were such a long, long time since we had been inside a house. It were really only a shack, but it seemed enormous to us. I think Becky were just curious, curious to know what sort of life she had left behind. She sat on the only chair while I touched the ashes of the fire. They were cold, so I knew the bounty hunter had been gone for days. She went into the other room where there were a bed and lied on it. She had a sort of sad expression when she got up, like she had lost something really important to her forever. I looked for food but there were none. Then I went back into the bedroom where I seen Becky staring into a shaving mirror. She were touching her muddy hair and face and running her fingers round the dried blood on her mouth. She bared her teeth and started to make growling, coughing sounds and then she opened up her mouth as far as it could go. She must have seen something terrible or hateful in the mirror cos she suddenly screamed and throwed the mirror against the wall. It shattered everywhere. She stared at the pieces on the floor for a moment and then ran out of the shack and back to the tigers, who were pacing up and down, real nervous.

We picked up as much of the dead sheep as we

could carry and set off home. We were nearing our den when we all stopped on account of hearing heavy footsteps. We rushed into the bracken and hid there. On top of a ridge we seen what looked like the silhouette of a half-man, half-beast. Looking closer I seen it were a man on a horse. It were too far to see his face but we hid cos we were so scared that he were the bounty hunter. Pretty soon he vanished over a hill. We picked up the sheep guts and lugged them back home. During the time it took to get back, Becky lagged behind, full of gloomy thoughts. One time I nuzzled her but she slapped me away. The tigers heard the slap and were puzzled. I sort of knew; the shack brought back thoughts of her father and home. She were terribly torn between being with us pack or wanting to try and find her father. She didn't join in eating the sheep carcass but sat outside on the cold, wet grass rocking back and forth, lost in her mind.

The female tiger's belly got bigger. Dave didn't like us touching her, but were all right 'bout us snuggling up to him. Corinna spent time by herself in the den. Becky began to return to her old self. I think she realised we needed each other now that the tigers were going to have pups.

We went hunting for Corinna cos we knew she needed food. Going on all fours had become natural to both me and Becky – not all the time, mind you. When we were in the den or outside we were on all fours and sometimes in a hunt we found ourselves running on all fours. As our hands and wrists became stronger we didn't even notice we were doing it. Corinna and Dave were our parents now and we copied them. But if it were a long chase – and sometimes that's the way we hunted, we'd chase after a wombat or young wallaby in a steady trot til it were worn out – it were easier to be on our two legs. The eyes of an animal we hunted to the point of exhaustion were always the same – I'd see surrender in their look. They'd given up all hope and were dying even before we killed them. It were as if they wanted to get it over and done with and be put out of their misery.

During the day Dave slept in the corner of the den by himself and Corinna slept nearby, but not cuddled up to us – now she was pregnant she seemed wary of Becky and me. Then one day she began to whimper real loud as if in pain and then her backside began to quiver and the male left the den. Corinna looked at us and growled and hissed so we skedaddled out into the watery day and sat shivering between the tree roots. We could hear her whimpering from inside and then she went quiet. I were afeared she were dead, so I peeked into the den and seen two tiny things no bigger than me finger crawling up into her pouch. She were licking them when she seen me. Her eyes told me to get back out, which I did quick smart.

When I joined Becky again Dave were gone, which were unusual cos it were day. He returned a few hours later, walking right past us – like we didn't exist. We peered into the den. He were vomiting up pieces of fur and meat for her and she were gobbling it all. Without even talking about it or thinking about it, we knew what we had to do. When Dave caught an animal or bird, we'd eat our fill, and then fill our gobs and crawl into the lair with our heads bowed, like kids with really strict parents, and vomit up our food for her. This won her trust and she allowed us to play with the pups when they could leave her pouch. She fed the two of them as she had fed me – from her teats. The pups just accepted us as part of their lives and sometimes when the parents went out hunting she'd leave them with us to look after. They were like dogs and we loved them. One were male, one were female. When they could walk we took them on short hunting trips where they could watch what we did. Most times they were lazy, just crowding up Corinna's pouch til they were so big they could no longer fit in.

It were in early summer that we went on a long hunting trip to a lake where the wallabies drank at sunset. It were a far way away, so the pups had to be strong enough. I think it were also a test to see how tough they were.

We walked through the night and arrived at the lake in the morning. It were a huge lake that went as far as the eye could see. It were so calm it were like a mirror and that meant I couldn't see below cos of the reflected clouds and bright morning sun. We picked some fronds and made a possie under an overhanging rock. Late afternoon we left the pups at the lair and we crept down through the grass and gum trees and waited. It were easy to hunt at the lake cos hundreds of wallabies came to drink. We saw a young one, a cocky one, that were by itself, sniffing the ground. There were two ways we killed. Either we trotted after our prey and followed it til it were so exhausted that it gave up, or we ambushed it. We were on the wallaby before it knew what were happening. It were like this explosion of panic cos once Dave were ripping open the throat of that young wallaby the whole tribe of them were scattering right, left and centre. The earth near the lake were pounding and bouncing up and down with the sounds of them running away. Oh, that *thump, thump, thump* of the earth, that got me heart thumping and me blood hot and bothered. Becky and me carried the dead wallaby back up the hill to the pups and we all ate together, like a true family again. I could feel me belly growing tighter and tighter as I filled me stomach. We were resting under the old man ferns, lazing about stuffed with food and contentment when Corinna decided to take the pups down to the lake cos their tongues were lolling out with the heat.

Becky were dozing and Dave were resting. I were watching the tigers by the lake as the sun were going down. I guessed Corinna were going to show her pups how to swim. Becky and I could do a dogpaddle but it were the tail that helped the tigers swim in the right direction and real quick. Compared to the tigers Becky and I swimmed real slow. I seen their three silhouettes as they drank from the water shiny with the setting sun. Then, like a nightmare, I seen a human, a man, moving slowly through the long grass and trees towards the tigers. I recognised him at once. It were that damned tiger man. He were like an evil spirit turning up. I seen he were carrying a rifle. I knew then what he were after. I barked a warning, real loud. Then again. I seen Corinna, who were standing in the water, looking up to where we were hidden in the old man ferns, and then she must have seen or heard something cos she looked up to where the man was taking aim. She ran towards her pups who were playing near the water's edge. A shot rang out and I seen a cub jump into the air and land dead still. Another shot rang out. Becky and Dave were now next to me, barking and coughing out warnings to Corinna. There were another shot just as she were 'bout to pick up the second cub by the scruff of the neck. The cub keeled over and it were dead too. Me heart were filled with screams but I couldn't open me mouth. Another shot rang out and I seen a puff of sand near Corinna. She paused and stared at her two pups and then seen the bounty hunter marching down towards her, reloading his rifle. She couldn't run towards us cos she knew she would have to pass right in front of the tiger man who were trying to kill her so she turned and raced into the water and swimmed away. He fired bullet after bullet at her but I could tell by the small sprays of water that the bullets were missing her. She swimmed right out and vanished into the twilight.

The tiger man looked down at the dead pups and then up towards us. I realised he must have seen me cos I were so upset that when I were warning Corinna I had stood up, clear above the scrub. He yelled out something and started to hurry up the hill towards us. We were terrified, so we ran back into the cover of the old man ferns and ran and ran on our two legs then on all fours til we were far away. He must have given up the chase, cos when we sneaked back he were gone. I could see Corinna creeping along the banks of the lake towards where her pups were. We ran down and joined her. There were nothing but some blood on the dirt and grass where the pups were shot. Corinna sniffed and sniffed, trying to pick up their scent. She sat down next to the bloodstains and remained there for hours. Near dawn she looked at us three with sad eyes and we knew it were time to go back home. And I also knew, through a kind of instinct and not me mind, that this had happened to her before. That's why she looked after us when she found Becky and me, cos her pups had been killed – probably killed by this same bounty hunter. Now she had no pups again. Only Becky and me were left.

On the way back I felt heavy with some darkness that were filling me mind just as the wallaby had filled me belly. Back in the lair Becky and I cried. Tigers don't cry, but they know sadness, they know emptiness, and both Dave and Corinna were empty except for sadness. Their eyes were glazed with sorrow; there is no other word for it. I'd say they were grief-stricken and so were me and Becky.

Corinna spent days, maybe weeks in the den. She grew thinner, even though her mate brought her food. Then one day she come hunting with us, and even though she didn't have much strength and gave up the chase after a quoll – which are devils to hunt cos they're so shy and quick – it were a sign she were getting better. We were closer than ever before, not only because of what happened to the pups, but because Becky and me were now like tigers too. Becky's language were fading, while all mine were gone. There were no reason to remember English any more. Words were no use to us when we were talking to the tigers, it were much easier to use our own language of grunts, growls, yawns, snuffles, coughing, looking, staring, so much so that if I'd mention the tigers to Becky, I'd call them 'Da' and 'Cor' – it were enough to understand who I were talking about. Me parents, well, they just slowly slipped out of me mind. They were like dreams, not real people.

One afternoon after we left the lair and were thinking about what direction to take to hunt, Dave rose up on his back legs to peer over some tall grass and daisy bushes and seen something that made his tail wag back and forth so quick like I had not seen before. I followed his gaze and seen another tiger moving towards Corinna who were standing there in the open just watching this tiger coming closer and closer. Dave began hissing like a snake and he ran through the bushes to the clearing. Becky and me ran to join him, knowing he were angry and spoiling for a fight. The other tiger were a male and he were moving in on Corinna. The two males faced each other. They were real cross, hissing and coughing, their stiff tails wagging back and forth not as a sign of happiness like in a dog but in anger. Then in a flash they were fighting and biting and snarling and growling. They chomped into each other, and tried to yawn as wide as possible so they could fit their jaws round the other's throat. I picked up some stones to throw at the other male, but Becky stopped me. She were like Corinna, strangely calm, while watching this – cos I s'pose they were confident that Dave would win the fight or they were resigned to whatever happened. The two tigers fought so wildly that soon they were raising a dust cloud. The wind got hold of the dust and it swirled round them like they were in a willy-willy of fury. There were blood on both of them and when their bodies hit the earth it shook with a loud thump. Sometimes they jumped away from each other, sucking in deep breaths, panting madly, with their tongues hanging right out, flies feasting on their bloody fur. Then they jumped back into the swirl. I knew that the two males were fighting over Corinna. I found meself yelling out *Da! Da!*, egging him on. After what seemed like hours, but it were probably only a few minutes, the other male backed away, looked at me and Becky and then at Corinna. He were covered in clouds of insects licking his blood. Maybe he decided it just wasn't worth it, cos all of a sudden he turned tail and limped away. Dave were weary and hurt too. Corinna licked his wounds and so did Becky and me. We helped him down to the creek where he drunked so much water I thought he might burst. Becky and me then washed the blood from him. He limped up to the lair and for several days lay there, eyes half closed, his weariness so deep that he dozed all day and night, trying to keep his eyes open just in case his enemy came back. But he never did. Dave were brave and Corinna knew it. She went out hunting by herself and brought back a rabbit for him. He were grateful – that were easy to see.

When I think back I see time were passing without me noticing. I lost me talking and lost me counting. It were the seasons I noticed: summer and autumn in the rainforests and hills and then winter down by the coast. We had four summers . . . That made me 'bout ten years old and Becky a bit more than eleven. Four years to a child is like an eternity. Every year I live now passes quicker and quicker but back then a year were an eternity so it were like a time without end.

Our world were a dark world. Most of our prey were creatures of the night like us. Sometimes at night it were like the whole of the bush were humming. There'd be the scratching, hunting, searching, fighting, snorting, barking, clicking noises of the dying bandicoots, the quolls, the mice, rabbits, dunnarts, possums, pademelons, grumpy wombats, swamp antechinus, potoroos, bettongs . . . it may be the secret dark world to humans but to me and Becky it were easy to see in. I knew what every silhouette, every shadow meant, no matter how quick the animal or bird were. Day were when animals hid in their burrows or in hollow trees, night were when we all came alive.

I learned what berries to eat if we were starving cos I watched what Dave and Corinna ate and most times the berries had no bad effect on me, but they could eat the native cherry til full while me and Becky threw up.

One sort of berry was so peppery that I dranked water for two days trying to cool my throat. Snowberries and purple berries were good to eat. We caught enormous crayfish in the creeks with our bare hands. If we couldn't find our usual prey then we hunted rats. They were tasty. We ate mushrooms that were like white tennis balls and a jelly shaped like an ear that growed on trees. We even ate goannas and skinks. If we wanted a pick-me-up we'd lick sassafras leaves.

I learned the countryside: the fens, the highlands of rock and stones, the rainforests, and what rivers we could cross. I saw orange-bellied parrots, wrens, wattle-birds, honey-eaters, currawongs, huge ravens and heard voices of a bird whose name I forget – it had a song like some-one whistling a jig. Then there were the smells: dung, rot, fresh kill, old kill, the devils smelling like lanolin, the gum trees reeking of peppermint, forest floors smothered in hairy toadstools that smelt of onion, then other toadstools that stanked of radish, fish, bitter almonds or even raw potato. There were special mushrooms that glowed in the night like hundreds of tiny lanterns. In summer the moors and fens were scarlet with flowers and the floors of the forests were white with petals of flowering gums and bushes. There were so much wattle that the countryside were yellow like someone had painted it during the night. Eyebrights and yellow bottlebrush and blue flowers stretched as far as I could see. It took a long time to learn the treachery of the earth – even Dave and Corinna were never a hundred per cent certain that the mossy ground we were walking on weren't a fake floor. You think you're walking on a real surface but it can gulp you up like it had tried to swallow Becky.

Difficult times were when it were bitter cold and prey weren't to be found, when the rain fell day after day til the whole forest were so sodden every step were a squelch. During these rainy times even our den were damp and all you could hear were the constant drip, drip, drip of water hours after it had stopped raining. It were aching hard on the legs to walk through those sodden forests, and it were wet country ripe for those damn leeches. Then there were the time I were bitten by a jack jumper. It were only a tiny ant but I fell into a coma and Becky had to drag me to the den where the three of them cared for me. Becky were afeared I'd die, til two days later I woke up. I can say at me ripe old age, with me knowledge and the experience I now have, that you haven't had a proper sting til you been stanged by a jack jumper.

I learned to read the eyes and body movements of the tigers and they learned mine and Becky's. It's why even now I can read a dog as easy as ABC. But there became a problem that Becky and I began to notice. The tigers tried to breed. The year after the bounty hunter killed her pups, Corinna had just the one cub but it died soon after birth. They tried more times but she never got pregnant again. Maybe it were the womb. Maybe after too many pups were killed the womb gave up.

A winter came that were more cruel than the ones before. The wind and hail were like sharp icicles cutting through me flesh. Even covering our bodies in mud didn't help and there were times when we didn't leave the lair because outside our skin turned prickly with goosebumps and our teeth chattered so much we couldn't growl or cough.

One day we were really desperate for food. Our prey were deep in their burrows and holes trying to keep the winter out, so we decided to try the bounty hunter's place again.

When we arrived, he had just got back himself with two fresh tiger carcasses. He carried them to the lean-to and then chopped some wood. His horse must have smelt us because it began to get antsy, tapping the earth with afeared hooves and pulling at its rope, trying to get away. The bounty hunter thought something was up and he hurried into the shack and came back outside with a rifle. Once we seen that, we were out of there, skedaddling as fast as possible down through the shrubs and running through the kerosene bush til we could run no more.

There were no other food available so we returned to the bounty hunter's to try and steal a sheep. His property were white with snow and smoke poured out of his chimney. He were home and therefore dangerous. But we were starving and we had no choice. It were hard to sneak up on the sheep cos Becky's and me feet squeaked on the hard snow, so we had to approach them real slowly and quietly, all the time keeping an eye open for the tiger man inside the shack who were singing a song at the top of his voice. The sheep were under the tree to shelter from the falling snow. Before they knew what was happening we snatched one and the rest of the sheep scattered. The tiger man must have heard their bleating cos he stopped singing. We had little time to lose and we dragged the sheep across the snow leaving a trail of blood. I thought I heard a door open and we stopped, our eyes agog. There were no sound of footsteps and me ears ached with trying to hear. Then he started singing again.

We ate much of the sheep when we were enough distance away and then lugged home the rest. A couple of days later we were outside the lair preparing to go hunting. It were a still, cloudless day and the winter sun were trying to warm us. We were feeling good, I remember that, and so we didn't feel the cold as much. We were moving through the snow across a ridge when I stopped. I smelt strange animals. I stood up, sniffed the cold air and looked over me shoulder. I couldn't speak cos I were stunned to see two men on horses and they were close. They were tiger men – I were sure of that.

I heard meself bark in fright and warning. The two men rode their horses through the snow across the ridge towards us. They were so fast that I just stood there in shock. Becky yelled out for us to run and she hightailed it to the lair. But cos I were afeared I kept slipping on the wet rocks and when I picked meself up after a fall I heard one of the men shouting. I turned and seen a man with a wild black beard, wearing an overcoat and carrying a rifle, leap off his horse and run at me. The other man, a fat one, slid off his horse and he too came at me. The tigers were coughing and barking and running in circles, alarmed by me and Becky's terror. The fat man slipped on a rock and fell into the snow, the other one were faster and thinner and he grabbed me. We both tumbled into the snow, but I jumped up first and as he tried to grab me again, I gave a threat yawn. But it didn't make him back off, so I threw meself at him, trying to bite his throat. He were screaming and the other man grabbed me from behind. I were also screaming and hissing like a devil. They were grunting with effort trying to hold me down. They were saying stuff I didn't understand and then the first man held me while the second ran across the snow to the lair. I barked out a warning to Becky. The fella holding me were struggling with me as I tried to escape. I barked to the tigers to help me and they started to circle us.

Out of the corner of me eye I seen the fat bloke pick up the rifle he had dropped in the snow and point it at the tigers. I felt meself filled with fury and I bit the hand that held the rifle. There was a sudden bang noise, like a clap of thunder, and we all stood still, shocked by the noise, then the tigers, knowing what the noise meant, ran off down the ridge, leaving me squirming with the fat fella. I heard the second man yell out something. He were standing at the opening to the den, then he crawled inside it. I heard Becky's horrible screams and cries and barks for help. The man came out dragging Becky like a rag doll. She were kicking and snarling and coughing, then she spit at him til his beard were twinkling in the sunlight with her spit, then somehow she managed to pull away and ran towards me. I yanked meself free of the fat man and Becky and me ran to each other and huddled together in the snow, panting, crying, fear running through our marrow. The two men circled us, staring at us. We didn't look at them, but into the distance – to where we would run to if we could escape. With a scream that pierced right through me, Becky jumped up and ran. The fat man threw himself at me and held me tight. The bearded man ran round in front of Becky, his arms stretched wide, crying out *Rebecca!* Becky stopped in her tracks and growled at him for a moment, then she went quiet as if really puzzled. I were puzzled too. The man knew her name. How did he know that? The two stared at each other in the panting silence til he grabbed her by the hand and led her back to me.

I were still jittery and eyeing for an escape. The man said something and touched me. I tried to move away but Becky held on to me. I didn't want eye contact with the man just in case he got angry with me. But I glanced at him and seen only a beard and hat. I caught Becky's eye and she knew what I were thinking – let's get out of here. I took off again, forgetting there were the other man nearby. He were fat but quick and he fell onto me, crushing me into the snow.

I s'pose they were worried that we would take any chance to run away, so we were tied to the packhorse with a rope, unable to move our hands. They had put some of their spare clothes on us. The trousers and shirt made me itch all over. I didn't struggle when they were putting them on cos I were stunned and shocked. But as they were tying me to the horse there were something familiar 'bout the bearded man's voice. It dawned on me that the older man whose face were hidden behind all that untamed hair were Becky's father, Mr Carsons.

He led the packhorse we were tied to, while the fat bloke rode behind us. We headed along the ridge. Halfway down it I heard a noise in snowy scrub nearby. Mr Carsons turned in his saddle, aimed his rifle and fired into the bushes. We jumped at the sound. He shot at the bushes again and the tigers ran from their hiding place down the other side of the ridge. Me and Becky coughed and barked out to them but they had skedaddled away. Mr Carsons said something to us. Becky and I looked at each other. We had no idea what he were going on 'bout. I were so not used to hearing people talk that it sounded like nonsense. Becky seemed to have gone into herself and looked so pale that she were as white as a winter's moon.

For three days and nights we travelled. For the first day I knew the tigers were following us. I seen them gliding through the mess of trees and shrubs. After that I seen them no more. I sniffed the air hard, as did Becky, but there were no familiar smells. They gave up on us, I s'pose. We were always tied up, whether it be on the packhorse or when we went to sleep round the campfire at night. Oh, that fire were so damn good. Sometimes Becky and

I got so close to it that the men had to drag us back from it. One time I fell into it and they had to pull me kicking and screaming while they slapped me noggin cos me hair were on fire.

The other man, the fat one, were clean-faced and younger than Mr Carsons. He sang and whistled when we rode, and at night he sang songs while we ate round the fire. His name were Ernest – he told us to call him Ernie. He laughed a lot. Mr Carsons had no laughter in him. He tried to cuddle Becky many times but she struggled away and when she did that he'd cry. I reckon she were already missing the tigers' fur and their smell. These two fellows stanked funny. It were a sort of stink like something really stale. Tigers smelt of the earth, the trees, the animals they ate and their spicy fur. These two fellas' stink were nothing like that – it were bitter and ugly.

I'd sit with Becky and we listened to the animals and birds of the night. There were the crackling leaves that meant a quoll were passing by. There were hissing and spitting in the distance as the devils had a brawl 'bout the animal they were eating. I could hear the owls and feel me blood go hot when I heard the squeal of the animals they catched. Becky's body went rigid when she heard it too. We were alive at night, all our nerves were sparking and prickly.

Mr Carsons were worried about us being awake at night, so he stayed up watching us and then the fat bloke woke to take his turn to guard us. We went to sleep near dawn and then snoozed on the packhorse as it made its way down the hills.

On the morning of the third day I seen a thin line of smoke in the distance and knew it were a house. We did not make for there, instead we took a trail through some trees and once they had thinned out we entered a huge valley. It were hotter now we were down from the hills. I seen some sheep and me stomach rumbled and me blood got excited. As we got closer I could see a house and barn. Mr Carsons turned round on his horse and said something to Becky. She did not answer. Maybe she wanted to but she didn't have the words for it any more.

As I peered over Becky's shoulder, cos she were in front of me, I remembered like it were a dream that I had seen this farm before. It were Mr Carsons's place. Becky were tied to me and I felt her body tremble like it were a fern in a violent wind. Mr Carsons got off his horse and walked the packhorse down the track through the front gate into the yard. Dogs ran out to greet him but on smelling us started barking like crazy. They jumped up at us so we snarled and barked back at them. They were scared shitless and skedaddled back to their kennel boxes, tails between their legs.

We rode towards the barn. Me blood got excited again when I seen chooks wandering round with no fear in their eyes. We stopped and Mr Carsons and the other bloke took us down from the packhorse. Once the dogs seen we were off the horse, they howled and barked and huddled up in a corner of the back yard. I smelled their fear and me body tingled with excitement. I also felt peculiar. I knew this were Mr Carsons's farm, cos I had seen it a couple of times, but I had forgotten it so it were new and strange to me now.

Still roped up, we were led to the verandah in the shade where we flopped down, exhausted and confused. I didn't know if Becky understood her father. He spoke to her a lot while Ernie were busy near the horse trough boiling water in a huge tin can on a fire. All I could understand in the mosquito buzz of Mr Carsons's words were *bzzz . . . Becky . . . bzzzz, Becky.* He kept on forcing her to look at him by holding her head like a vice and turning it towards him, but she coughed and opened her jaw, letting him know she did not want eye contact. We had learnt not to do that, cos it makes a tiger angry.

Before we had time to recover, the men took off our clothes and carted us to the trough. We were struggling cos we didn't know what were happening. Ernie had poured the hot water into the trough. When I seen that water and felt the men's strong arms trying to push us in, well, I barked, coughed and gave them a threat yawn, but they still shoved me in. I can see now how filthy we must have been. We were a mess of bruises, scars and calluses, especially on our hands and knees. Our hair were dirty, so dirty that Becky's blonde hair were black. The men were trying to calm us with their words and firm grip. It were like torture as they soaped us. I could take no more and bit one of the men's hands – I have no idea whose hand. The grip went weak and I jumped out of the trough and started running. There were a right kerfuffle with yelling, shouts and barking – and howling from the scared dogs – as I made a run for it. I seen the far cloudy mountains and I set out for them.

I had only taken a few steps when I slipped in the mud and Ernie dived on me. We rolled in the mud. I tried to bite his face but he slapped me hard. He carried me back to the trough. Just as he threw me back into it Becky took the opportunity to leap out but she slipped in the mud too. Her father caught her and put her back in with me. They washed us clean and then took us onto the verandah to dry us. I felt naked, not cos I weren't wearing clothes but cos I didn't smell like meself any more. It were as if me real clothes had been taken from me. I smelt raw like a skinned sheep.

Mr Carsons went inside and returned with two women's nightdresses and after measuring them against us, and finding them too large, he cut off the ends and dressed us in them. Then he tied a rope round our waists. The dogs continued to howl and bark. I wanted to go and piss in the yard to leave me scent to put the fear of God into them, but we were taken inside. The house reminded me of the bounty hunter. To me the insides of a house were where killers lived. I were stubborn and tried to resist but Ernie were strong. We were taken down a corridor and I followed Mr Carsons and Becky into a room.

It were dark and Mr Carsons pulled open the curtains. There were a bed and some furniture. He guided Becky to a dressing table and showed her a photograph of him with a woman and a baby. He said something, asked her something, but she had no clue what he were talking about and she looked to me as if I might understand, but I had no idea either. Then she suddenly let out a shout and jumped back from her twin. Me too, I were shocked. I had seen meself reflected in the water when I drank it but Becky and I had forgotten about mirrors and we found ourselves growling at her twin til it dawned on us that the twin were not real – she were only Becky.

I were sorely in need of rest. It were the middle of the day. Mr Carsons seemed upset by Becky's reaction to the photograph, and seeing we were yawning with tiredness took us outside onto the verandah and tied us to the railing. We balled up together, seeking warmth and comfort, and went to sleep. It were a fitful sleep. We kept waking up on hearing footsteps on the verandah floor, the clucking of chooks and the bleating of sheep.

Round twilight the two men took us into the kitchen. Ernie put me on a chair. It felt hard on me bum and I slid off it onto the floor. He tried to lift me up on it again but I made meself feel like a rag doll and I slid off again. He gave a big sigh and left me on the floor. Mr Carsons told Becky to sit. She just stood. He pushed her onto a chair. She squealed like a quoll being attacked and plopped down on the floor next to me. He tried to lift her back in the chair again but when he stepped away she just flopped down next to me. He gave up after that.

They gave us some food. It were hot and tasted like charcoal. I spat it out, so did Becky. It were a dreadful taste. Then I knew what we wanted. We wanted raw meat. We wanted energy. We wanted fresh meat and, if the truth be known, the taste of blood. Ernie tried to put some food into me mouth. I spat it out and Becky started to tear off her shift. It were so funny as she growled and tore at it that I laughed meself sick. Then she stopped right in the middle of her fury and listened. I stopped laughing and listened too. We could hear a faint scurrying and then a mouse appeared in the far corner and fled back behind the wall. Becky growled a command to me. I knew what that meant: *Let's skedaddle.* We jumped up and raced out on all fours into the night and freedom.

We ran down the dark corridor to a door, but it were locked. We turned to go the other way and seen Ernie, surprisingly fast for one so big, race to the other entrance to block it off. Both men were yelling for us to stop. Ernie came at us. We ran back and stopped halfway in the corridor. We were panting with excitement and panic. I looked into a side room. Becky knew, for we could talk without words, that I had seen an escape route.

It were the parlour window we made for. It were opened and we jumped through it and onto the grass. I heard the two men running down the corridor and outside into the back yard. Becky and I looked round. Where to go? There were a fence ahead of us, but there were also a small track down the side of the house that led to a gate we could easily get over. We set off on all fours again, not realising cos we were so wound up that we weren't listening properly. I thought the men were behind us, but one had gone round the side of the house and came straight at us. It were Mr Carsons. We tried to turn back but there – ready for us – were Ernie.

We were tied up to a bed. We couldn't undo

the knots cos our fingers wouldn't work. Becky tried to chew through the ropes, it only made her gums bloody. We were trapped. It were like being in a prison. We howled and growled. We listened without breathing, hoping the tigers would call out to us, but heard only silence.

Next morning we were drowsy from lack of sleep. The two men carted us outside where they had made a strange contraption. There were two, made of leather and tied by a rope to a pepper-tree branch. They put us into a contraption each. It were like a straitjacket that kept us hanging upright, our toes just touching the earth. We swang back and forth for what seemed like hours and the men gradually lowered the ropes, keeping us upright til our feet touched the ground, but we were still hanging. Mr Carsons untied Becky and she stood upright and began to walk. The two men cried out in gladness at what they seen. They untied me but it felt strange to put so much weight on me feet that I fell to the earth. Becky seen me on all fours and joined me, much to the woe of the two men.

Again and again they put us in the contraption to make us try and stand on two feet. Most times we just swang back and forth from the tree, dozing through the hot day, sometimes waking on hearing a chook or the bleating of sheep out in the paddocks. We were awful hungry.

Late in the day Carsons did some work round the barn. I woke up when I seen him throw some meat and bones to the dogs. Ernie were asleep in a cane chair on the verandah. I kicked Becky awake and she seen what I did – the bones and meat. Mr Carsons had gone round the back of the barn. Me ropes were slack and I wiggled free, then I helped Becky. Ernie were still snoring away. We raced across the yard to the dogs. They howled and scattered. We pounced on the animal carcass they were eating. Oh, the yard were full of dogs barking and howling, chooks squawking, roosters cockadoodling and Becky's father yelling at Ernie. By the time the two men had got to us, we had gobs full of meat. Mr

Carsons grabbed his daughter and Ernie held me. Mr Carsons were real angry and slapped Becky on the legs – she didn't cry out, our bodies had been made hard.

They put us back in the slings. We hadn't eaten proper food for days. We needed meat, fresh meat at that. Every day the two men would put us in the slings and hang us from the pepper tree and they'd try to get us to walk upright. But the thing were – we were too dead beat to do anything that meant effort. We were thinning. We were starving. I think Ernie knew and I seen him staring at us and rubbing his shiny chin as if thinking real deep 'bout us. One morning he guided Mr Carsons out to where we were lying on the verandah. They stared down at us. I couldn't see Mr Carsons' reactions cos of his black beard but I seen his eyes and they seemed hurt as he looked long and hard at us. Then he nodded, said something, and went into the house, coming back out with a rifle. He headed off into the nearby scrub and not long afterwards we heard a couple of shots.

Our eyes were keen and we could see him returning through the scrub and wattle trees with a small wallaby. O me, O my, how excited were we. I knew, Becky knew, that the wallaby were for us. We were so jittery with eagerness that we swang back and forth and round in the pepper tree like we were storm-tossed. Mr Carsons walked right past us while Ernie brought out a meat safe. Instead of giving us the wallaby, Mr Carsons cut it up and shoved it in the meat safe. At this point I were starting to be cranky. On another bough of the pepper tree Ernie rigged up the meat safe to a rope so it hung there smelling of warm blood and meat. Now I were really cranky like Becky were and we were growling and coughing and giving both men the stare and opening our jaws real wide to show them we were angry.

Finally we were released from the slings but still tied to ropes. We reached up for the meat but it were too far above us. Carsons touched the safe handle and guided Becky underneath it. She coughed with frustration as she tried to reach the meat and then her father lifted her up onto her legs. She stood up and reached for the handle. I knew what her father were doing. He were trying to make us stand up and not be on all fours like an animal.

He helped her turn the handle then he grabbed some meat and threw it to her. She ate like it were her last meal. Ernie did the same thing to me and it took every effort for me weak legs to hold me up but with the help of Ernie I reached the handle. I pulled and pulled at it and began to cry with frustration til Ernie opened the door for me. I needed no second chance. I reached in and grabbed a hunk of meat. Ernie let me go and I fell to the ground. I were 'bout to eat when I heard Becky's soft growling and crunching. I looked and seen her in the shade of the verandah tied to one of the posts gobbling down her meat. I ran to her as fast as my chain – held by Ernie – could take me.

That day is so clear in me head. We were famished and just ate and ate while the two men watched us with a mixture of curiosity and disgust. There were so much blood and meat muck on us when we finished that they stripped us naked and hosed us down. We didn't care, cos we were full up to dolly's wax. We were buzzing with life as dusk came – that's how much fresh meat pucked us full of energy.

We stayed awake on the verandah listening to the dark. Even though we were tied up, the men took it in turns to watch us through the night. Near dawn I thought I heard a snuffle in the bush outside the front fence. Becky looked at me. She must have heard it too. We listened real careful but the sound were gone. We stayed alert but there were nothing more.

We were curled up together sleeping when we were woken up and taken into a bedroom. I were yawning and not in a happy mood and nipped Ernie's hand. He yelped like a dog and stayed his distance from me. Mr Carsons undressed Becky. She were naked and looked to me as if to say, *What's happening, Hannah?* Her father tried to put a blue dress on her but she squirmed and whimpered. I seen it were too tight, but her father and the fat man squeezed it onto her. She tried to pull it off but her father kept on shouting, *No!* He were very firm with her. He dragged her in front of a full-length mirror and asked her some questions. She did not answer but stared at herself like she were seeing a stranger. She took a step closer and really looked at herself. She stroked the dress as if she recognised it and frowned like she had all the thoughts in the world whirling through her.

They tried to put a dress on me. I couldn't hack it. There were a kerfuffle and once I ripped off the dress the men gave up. I gave Ernie a threat yawn when he came towards me holding another frock. Becky gave a peculiar smile when I did me yawn, like she were looking down on me for some reason I couldn't work out; it were like she thought she were better than me. Her father went out of the room and came back with a shirt and trousers. He measured the pants against me and then picked up a pair of scissors and cut them to me size. The shirt were loose on me and so were the trousers which Ernie tied round me with a piece of string. I felt free compared to Becky. She couldn't run in her dress unless she lifted it up, and she had to walk slower with smaller steps.

The men were pleased with what they had done and took us into the living room where there were a piano and a mechanical contraption Ernie were putting together with a box and a horn like a funnel 'bout six feet long. I were going to sit on the floor when I seen a movement out of the corner of me eye. I felt like playing, so I jumped at a string swinging back and forth across the window. I held it by me teeth and pulled. It gave way and I fell backwards in fright as the stick holding the curtains broke and they fell on top of me. There were yelling and shouting, but once I seen that it were only the curtains, I grabbed them by me teeth and dragged them round and round the room chased by the two men. Becky were laughing and I were inwardly laughing too. It were great fun. Once they caught me they tore the curtains from me hands and tied me up again.

The ropes were tight so I could tell Ernie were getting angry with me. I looked to Becky to help me but she were staring at the piano. Her father seen what she were doing and opened up the lid. She had that frown again. She stepped right up to it and bent down and sniffed it, then she touched a key with her nose. The sound of the note made her jump back in surprise. Her father said something soothing. It calmed her and she reached out and touched a note with her finger. It made a sound, then she touched another one and another one. It sounded like icicles breaking off and other times like an animal were making a threat.

She stopped and looked round at us three, her eyes wide with amazement. She remembered it! She remembered playing the piano: that much were plain. Her father told her to sit on the piano stool but she kicked it away and started to thump at the keys with all the energy she could muster. It were like she were playing music that were inside her head, like she were imitating the noises of tigers and devils. It were exciting music to me so I howled along with it and she howled too til her father shouted out above the racket: *Rebecca!*

She span round like she heard a shot. He kept repeating her name in a quieter voice. She listened carefully, her head on a tilt. The two men stared so close at her it were like their eyes were drilling right into her to feast on her brain. Then Becky mouthed the word: *Re-becc-a.* The men egged her on. She said it again and her father laughed with excitement and so did Ernie. She said her name again and again til her father shushed her. Becky were joyful cos she made her father happy. She went back to playing the piano, humming away and making rooster sounds to the nonsense tunes she were making. I pretended I were a rooster too. I liked rooster cock-a-doodle-dooing cos I think it were funny.

Ernie stopped me crowing and pushed me to the table on which he had put his machine. Mr Carsons stopped Becky from playing and placed her next to me. I were curious about this machine. I couldn't make head or tail of it, but I sensed that the men wanted us to use it or play with it. He hummed what Becky had been singing and pushed us close to the big funnel. Ernie turned a handle and a needle dropped onto a black cylinder that started to spin. Becky realised her father wanted her to sing what she were singing at the piano, so she hummed her song into the funnel. Her father tapped me on the back and I realised he wanted me to join in. Becky and me did this for 'bout a minute and then we were told to stop. It all seemed peculiar to me and to Becky, who looked to me as if to say: *Do you understand any of this?* I had to shake me head.

We were told to sit on chairs but Becky copied me by just flopping down on the floor near the table to wait for another silly request from these two ginks. I were thirsty and thinking about water when Ernie clapped, wanting us to pay attention to him. He turned the handle of the machine. I heard a voice that were singing like Becky. I looked at her but her mouth were hanging open in surprise and wonder. Then I recognised me own voice coming from inside the machine. How had our voices got into that machine? We both ran to the table to find the answer. Becky's father held us back from touching the funnel. Becky grew really anxious and were shaking her head saying, *No, no, no!* I were trying to reach out and find me voice inside that infernal contraption. Our voices had been stolen! Someone had stolen me! I stared at the needle on the turning cylinder and realised our singing were in there. I wanted to smash it. It were spooky. It were magic. Ernie pushed me back when I reached out to smash the cylinder that had stolen our voices. I gave him the biggest threat yawn ever, as did Becky who seen what I were trying to do and she agreed with me. We were both in a panic wanting our voices to escape from that cylinder prison. She broke free and ran out the room. Ernie was protecting the machine so I were able to run out the room too.

I were hightailing it down the corridor after Becky and then we both skedaddled outside onto the verandah. I continued to run when I noticed that Becky were no longer beside me. I looked back and seen her standing on the edge of the verandah with that frown of hers. Her father and Ernie stopped chasing us and walked up behind her, standing side by side with her as the three of them looked at me. Mr Carsons stepped down off the verandah and called me by me name. Then he pointed to Becky, as if to say, *She is staying, why don't you?* I looked round and seen the forest and mountains in the distance.

Becky! I called out, wanting her to come with me but she were staying put like her feet were nailed to the verandah floorboards. What could I do? I didn't want to run away by meself. Becky were me closest person in the whole world.

I joined her on the verandah and she rubbed her face against mine and the world were fine then. It must have been something about me panic that made Mr Carsons realise he had to do something for me, cos a little while later the four of us were in the buggy riding out of the front gate, the horse jittery maybe cos it sensed we two girls smelt different from other humans.

We rode for several hours down dirt tracks and then along the river bank for some miles. The two men were worried 'bout us escaping, so we were tied together and Ernie held the ropes while Becky's father drove. It were wonderful to be so inside the bush. It felt like home: the trees, the smells of animals and shit, the flowers and the gums.

Then something happened inside me: I began

to recognise, like a dream that becomes real, the countryside we were travelling through. Me heart went racing and I sweated. I realised Mr Carsons were taking me to me real home, me parents' home. I tried to stand in the buggy I were so excited, but Ernie pulled me down. Memories of me mother and father swirled round me mind. I only had Becky's word that me mother were drowned and as for me father she hadn't seen him dead, so I was filled to the brim with the belief that they were still alive and I would see them again.

And there it were! I recognised the house as we drove up the overgrown path. I struggled to free meself. Ernie untied me ropes as we neared me home. I jumped out of the buggy and ran towards it. It seemed the same, but as I raced up the front steps a rotted one gave way and I fell. I didn't care that I were bleeding from me chin, and after pushing open the door ran inside hearing meself call out *Mummy ... Daddy ...* Frightened mice and possums ran across the floors or scrambled up into the ceiling. Me face were soon sticky with cobwebs. I ran from room to room, but there were no one, only putrid couches and curtains. I ran into me parents' bedroom. The bed were still there with the bed covers splattered with possum and rat shit. A fraying corset were on the mannequin. When I seen the rotting bedroom I knew me mother and father were dead. I couldn't hack it. I fell to the floor and wept. I heard footsteps behind me. Then I felt Becky hugging me, cradling me, nuzzling me, as she rocked me back and forth while I wept for me parents and meself. I knew deep down that I had no one, no one except for that girl comforting me.

I can't remember the trip back to Mr Carsons's farm. I were a shell of meself. If you had whacked me, all you would have heard would be a hollow sound as if you had hit an empty drum. I were put on the verandah. There were no need to tie me up now – both men knew that. They knew that I would stay wherever Becky were and she wanted to stay on the farm, I sensed that, I knew that.

I were so inside meself I didn't notice til the last minute that Ernie were leaving. He had a packhorse with his machine tied to it and I only seen he were going when he stopped beside me and whispered something – which sounded kind – and ruffled me hair. He were a gentle man, I sensed that. When he hopped on his horse Becky patted the box which held the machine. *There, there . . .* she said. I knew what she were doing; she were calming down our song inside the box.

I watched Ernie slowly ride out the front gate with Mr Carsons walking beside him, talking 'bout something. Me mother and father had gone and now Ernie were gone. I wanted to howl like a dog. I wanted to claw at me body. I seen a pool of water in the mud near the horse trough and I don't know why but I ran towards it, tearing off me shirt and trousers on the way. I rolled in the mud, weeping, feeling the comfort of the warm mud on me skin. I wanted to return to the tigers. I wanted to be a tiger. I were demented – no doubt about that – and

I grabbed some mud and tried to draw stripes on me back. I heard Becky making soothing sounds in me ear. I heard me name being called by Mr Carsons, but I didn't care, I were weeping and howling so much. Then I felt her fingers on me skin. Becky were drawing stripes on me back with the mud. I stopped weeping. It felt calming. I opened me eyes and seen Mr Carsons watching us in the mud. He didn't try to stop what his daughter were doing to me. Becky were snuffling as she did the stripes and when she finished she laughed with delight. That caused me to laugh too. I didn't feel so alone now. I were sad, sad to my marrow, but I had Becky. After sitting in the warm mud for some time she stood up and helped me to the trough where we bathed together in the cold water, teeth chattering, me skin like the goosebumps of a plucked chook. After we were clean Mr Carsons took us inside and fed us freshly killed possum.

Cos Mr Carsons knew that I wouldn't run away without Becky he allowed us to roam free round the farm as long as we didn't scare the chooks or dogs. One night while I were sitting on the verandah peeking into the darkness hoping Corinna and Dave would turn up, Becky came outside wearing a new dress. She sat on the cane chair near where I were on my haunches. We had both stopped walking on all fours but I didn't take to sitting on chairs cos they were too hard for me arse. Becky were becoming different. She liked sitting in chairs now. There were something about her mood that didn't sit well with me. It were like she were smiling down at me from her chair. It were a look I had seen that once before, like she were better than me. I gave her a threat yawn. She laughed and pointed to herself, saying, *Becky*. She pointed to me and said, *Hannah.* I knew me name. I didn't need her telling me I were stupid. I growled at her but she paid no attention cos her eyes were on a frog hopping across the verandah floor. Her hand jumped out and she caught it in the middle of its leap. She got up and went inside. I were lonely, so I followed her.

She walked down the corridor and went into the bedroom where Mr Carsons were dozing. I peered round the door and seen her slowly approach her father who were lying on his back, his eyes suddenly open, knowing his daughter were in the room. Her eyes were radiant, as the dim light of his bedroom were perfect to see in. She snuffled and moved towards him. I could see dread in his eyes. I think he were wondering if Becky were going to kill him. She stopped at the side of the bed and jumped at him. He sat bolt upright, his eyes bright with terror. Becky laughed. I knew she were playing a game with him only he didn't know. She looked surprised at his reaction and she gave him a nuzzle. He didn't know what to make of this but he didn't push her away. He allowed her to snuffle, lick and nuzzle him. She touched him on the face and began to speak. It were as if she were stuttering at first, saying *d-d-d-d-d* til she paused and then whispered *Daddy*. She grinned and he smiled in return. She opened her left hand and the frog fell onto the bed, surprising her father, before it began to hop across the blanket; it were her gift for him. She nuzzled him as he stroked her hair. They were real close then and I were not.

Every day after that Becky seemed to grow further from me. Her father taught her to speak again. He got me to sit in on her lessons but I were not interested. I didn't feel the need to speak. I knew what a few words meant, like *food, dog, sheep* and *gun* but I didn't speak, unlike Becky who ate up all the learning. She were so caught up in it that if she got a word or sentence wrong she would slap her forehead and call herself stupid. Becky wanted to speak like she did before. She wanted to change. She tried real hard, like I hadn't seen her before. She were the type that were always yes or no. If she wanted something real hard, she tried real hard.

Even when she weren't learning or reading she were playing the piano instead of being with me. I think I began to be worried that she were separating herself from me cos me skin broke out in sores something bad. I picked at them and pretty soon I were covered in scabs. Mr Carsons tried to stop me from picking at them but I couldn't help it. I felt anxious and bothered all the time. Other things were changing with Becky. She began to sleep at night. This really worried me cos I were awake at nights still. One evening I went into her bedroom where she were sleeping and I grabbed her hand with me teeth and tried to pull her on her feet but she slapped me away. She didn't want to sleep when it were daytime. She said dogs did that, people didn't.

I spent a lot of time at night by meself. I liked sitting on the roof and listening to the sounds and noises of owls, squealing mice, fighting devils, the quolls running across dry grass and the spitting of possums – all of this wrapped up in the lovely scents of flowers in the night summer breeze.

Becky started to eat cooked meat on a plate with a knife and fork. I ate raw meat and sat on the kitchen floor. One day Becky gave me that strange stare again – one where she looked down on me – and she mimicked the noises I made when I ate and the way I didn't close my mouth when I chewed. I gave her a threat yawn but she only laughed. Mr Carsons, sitting at the table with Becky, told me to stop. I were angry so I spat meat on his boots. He cried out, *Oh my God!* I laughed at him cos it seemed he were too serious 'bout what I had done. It were so funny that I found meself mimicking him. The first time I were just making sounds and then something happened inside me head. I heard meself and realised that I hadn't mimicked him properly so I said, clear as a bell, *Oh my God . . . Oh my God . . .* It struck me – I could talk! Oh, I'll go bail if I didn't drove those two mad for the rest of the day, just saying over and over, *Oh my God . . .* like some magic incantation. And it were magic cos I were speaking, even Becky were impressed.

Later in the evening I were watching Mr Carsons put a freshly shot joey in the meat safe that hung from the pepper tree when I heard the faint sound of a sheep bleat in the distance. Becky heard it too, cos she turned in the direction of the sound like I did. It bleated in terror. I heard Mr Carsons ask his daughter what she were listening to, but Becky didn't answer. She knew what it were, like me. Me heart beat fast with happiness. We shared a look and both of us knew what we were hearing and we took off, not obeying Mr Carsons who were calling us back. His cries telling us to stop could barely be heard over the barking and yelping of the dogs.

We leapt over the front yard gate and ran through the long grass towards where we heard the sheep being killed. I coughed and keened like a tiger but there were no answer. We found Mr Carsons's prize ram, bright scarlet in the moon-light, its skull crushed and its brain eaten. It were tigers all right. But were they Corinna and Dave? I peered real hard into the darkness and seen two fire-bright eyes staring back at us 'bout a hundred yards away. It were a tiger and it stanked of male. Becky and I coughed and keened then we seen the silhouette of a tiger turn and come towards us. We jumped in fright when we heard a shot whistling past us. It were Mr Carsons shooting at the tiger. The bullet missed and the tiger hightailed it back into the dark bush. Becky's father gave a large sigh when he seen the dead ram. It were the sigh of a disappointed man. I caught a glimpse of the tiger racing over the hill and made a howl of distress. Mr Carsons slapped me across the leg, telling me to stop. He grabbed Becky's arm. He were in a desperate, angry mood and asked her if it were a girl or boy tiger. She told the truth – it were a boy.

Next morning Mr Carsons were up very early. He spent nearly the whole day digging a trench in the paddocks. I had no idea why he were doing it, nor did I care. I lied in the sun on the verandah catching up with me sleep while Becky played the piano over and over, the music sounding less . . . less jangled and nervous, more soft and gentle, and it had – if I had known the word then – melody.

When we had finished our tea, Mr Carsons tied

us up to the verandah railings again. *Why?* Becky kept asking when he bounded her to one of the posts. He didn't reply and put a gag round her mouth. He were very serious and had a great purpose in mind – that were easy to tell. What were Mr Carsons doing? I thought to meself. He gagged me, but instead of tying me to a verandah post he pulled me across the paddock to the trench, and after tying me wrists together, lifted me down into it. Only if I stood on me tiptoes could I see over it. Then he covered the top of the trench with a frame of branches, leaves and grass. I heard him walk away and I were left alone. I were frightened and confused – the trench were like a grave. I were in a dark hole with only bits and pieces of moonlight shining through the lid of leaves and branches above me.

After an hour I sat down. I had no idea how long Mr Carsons were going to keep me in the trench. Were he going to kill me? I wondered to meself. Maybe I had done something wrong. But what? I were feeling sad for meself when I smelt a tiger coming closer. I stood up on my toes and pushed me head through the branches. I smelt him first before seeing him, it were Dave. I tried to make noises but me mouth were gagged with a scarf. I seen Dave push his nuzzle through the lid sniffing as hard as possible and then suddenly it were all chaos. He fell through the lid onto me. We were rolling round trying to stand up in the mess of leaves and branches when I heard Mr Carsons running towards the trench and a moment later there he were looking down at us and pointing his rifle at Dave. He reached down with his free hand and lifted me out of the trench.

I flopped down beside the trench. Mr Carsons pointed his rifle down at Dave who were trying to jump out of the trench, and fired three bullets into him. Exactly three – those three shots were like me being stabbed in me heart three times. I crawled to the side of the trench and looked down. Dave were lying there, his eyes closed, his flanks bleeding. He were dead, that were easy to tell. I found meself saying over and over, *Oh my God,* even when Mr Carsons were taking me back to the verandah where Becky were howling with grief and trying to bite the ropes to free herself. Mr Carsons tried to calm her but she tried to bite him even though she still wore a gag. She were furious with her father as I were. I were in a fury of teeth-gnashing and weeping. Dave had helped save us. He and Corinna had cared for us. We had hunted with them. They were our father and mother. Now Dave were murdered. That's how I thought of it – Becky's father had cold-bloodedly murdered Dave and used me as bait to attract him cos he knew the tigers cared for me. That's why Dave sniffed me out and came for me.

We refused to eat for four days. Mr Carsons kept us tied up cos he were afeared that we would run away. Becky didn't want to talk or play piano, she were grieving like me. He tried to talk to his daughter but she gave him the threat yawn or bared her teeth and growled. He tried to get her to read and play piano, but she tore up the books and spat on the piano keys. She told her father she hated him. It were now his turn to weep. He spent much of the time lying on his bed, his eyes full of misery.

It were me who seen Ernie first. I were listening to me stomach grumble while I lied with Becky on the verandah when I smelt horses. One was a packhorse loaded with boxes while the other had a rider. He were fat. He were Ernie. He rode into the back yard and after getting off his horse he greeted us with a nuzzle. He were puzzled as to why we were so weary. He didn't know we hadn't eaten for days. He called out for Mr Carsons and when he got no answer he went inside.

What followed were a strange week. Mr Carsons spent most of the time in bed and Ernie cared for us. Becky had gone back to sleeping of a day and staying awake with me through the night. Ernie bounded us up so we wouldn't escape cos he knew that we were being called by the bush. We were desperate to find Corinna. He fed us and spent time in Mr Carsons's room talking gently to him – Becky's father seemed stricken by some inner sickness. Left to ourselves we didn't sit on chairs any more but on the floor. Becky and me were now back being close. We were with each other all day and night.

Gradually Mr Carsons spent less time in bed. I think Ernie were trying to change his mind 'bout something. Sometimes he'd take Mr Carsons's hand and have him come and stare at us and they'd talk softly about things I didn't understand. The only thing that began to change were that Mr Carsons shook his head a lot when talking to Ernie and then one morning, while we were eyeing the chooks and the two men were looking at us, I seen out of the corner of me eye Mr Carsons nod his head once and after Ernie said something to him, he nodded his head up and down til I thought it were going to fall off.

The next morning Becky and I were in the buggy with Mr Carsons and Ernie were on his horse accompanying us. For the first few hours I thought I could smell a female tiger following us but I didn't know if I were dreaming it or not. We passed through thick forests and bush til the bush became paddocks filled with sheep and cattle and the tracks became a wide road at the end of which was a distant mountain with snow on it. We travelled over a hill and there in front of us were thousands of houses surrounding a harbour filled with ships. *Hobart*, said Ernie. It meant nothing to me.

It were early morning and the city were asleep. A thick mist made it hard to see where we were going. It seemed like we were the only people alive and the hooves and wheels of the buggy sounded loud and harsh on the cobbled streets. Both me and Becky were gobsmacked by how large and scary were this town. It smelt different too; of chimney smoke, horse shit and rotting fish.

When we arrived in the centre of Hobart, Ernie rode off with his packhorse and Mr Carsons took us to a hotel. Once we were in a room he washed and bathed the both of us. He put Becky in a new dress, and some old trousers and shirt on me cos he knew

I would tear up any dress they tried to put me in. He were hurrying and were up to a purpose. While I were pondering just what this hard man were on 'bout, he grabbed me, tied me up to a chair and put a gag round me mouth. He did it with anger cos I think deep down he blamed me for what happened to his daughter. Becky tried to stop him but he slapped her hands away and despite her threat yawn told her in a stern, no-nonsense way that he had to be obeyed. His gaze were so strong and his voice so tough that she stopped trying to rescue me. He took her to the door. I cried out her name from the bottom of my heart, sensing they were taking her from me but it must have sounded like I were merely coughing cos no real words escaped from the prison me mouth now were in. Becky tried to say something to me but her father shoved her into the hallway before slamming the door behind him.

What words can I use for how I felt? I had this fist of terror in my heart. I knew he were taking her from me. I managed to stand up with the chair still strapped to me bum and get meself to the window. I looked down and seen a white-faced Becky in the buggy next to her father. I hit my face against the window trying to get her attention, but she must have been in a state of shock or maybe she didn't hear. Her father cracked his whip and the buggy drove off and as it did Becky turned round and looked up at me. She were weeping and so were I.

I watched the buggy vanish into the fog. I had to find where it had gone. I rocked from side to side on me chair trying to free meself. It took me an hour but I managed to wiggle out of the ropes. I tried the door but it were locked. There were no way out except for the windows. The problem were I didn't know how to open them. I tried to lift one up but it were locked with a piece of metal like the wings of a butterfly. I were beside myself with desperation so I picked up the chair and smashed it against the window. It shattered and I looked out, but it were clear that if I jumped down into the street I would hurt meself so I crawled onto the ledge and reached out for a drainpipe. Once I grabbed it I were able to shimmy me way down til I were close enough to jump onto the ground. After I got me bearings, I chased after the buggy in the direction I thought it had gone.

Pretty soon I were lost. I sniffed the air and smelt something familiar, something that brought back memories of me father. I followed the smell and found meself down at the wharf. There were a ship there and men were carrying boxes and food up the gangplank. I had an eerie feeling that the ship had something to do with me father. After a time I recognised the stink that coated the ship – it were the smell of whales, that clung to me father's skin for weeks when he came home from the sea. I were so caught up in the feeling that the ship had something to do with me father that I didn't hear a buggy arrive. It were Mr Carsons and Ernie. They had been looking for me. I asked them where Becky were. They said nothing. I pointed to the ship and told them that me father were on a ship. I don't think they heard me right and Mr Carsons asked if

I wanted to board the ship to find me father. I were shivering with a sense of losing Becky and me father so I weren't thinking straight and I had this fancy that he were alive.

While Ernie waited with me, Mr Carsons went on board. He disappeared for half an hour and then came out onto the deck with the captain and pointed to me. The captain stared at me for a long while, like he were debating something with himself and then the two men shook hands. Mr Carsons joined us and we drove back to the hotel. Ernie took me up to the room while Mr Carsons went off to do something. Ernie cut me hair and said that me name was Harry. I shook me head. Me name were Hannah. Mr Carsons came back with some clothes he had buyed for me. They were boys' trousers and shirts and boots. They knew I didn't like shoes or boots, but they forced them on me. They had me walk round the room many times with fat Ernie miming how I should walk. I soon picked up that they wanted me to walk like a boy. They acted out for me how to walk tough. They were talking to me about something I didn't understand when Mr Carsons said to Ernie, *Show Harry*. With that Ernie pulled down his trousers. I almost fainted when I seen his huge privates under a ledge of fat. Then, without warning he pulled down my trousers. They looked at me quim and shook their heads. I didn't get it. They did it again, only this time they put their hands over their eyes and shook their heads. They clicked their tongues with irritation and Ernie pulled up my trousers again and pointed to his privates. I felt like a dog being taught a trick I didn't understand the reason for. Ernie pulled up his own trousers and then yanked down mine. They covered their eyes and shook their heads again. The penny dropped – they didn't want people to know I were a girl.

They took me down to the ship as it were preparing to sail. Captain Lee were there to greet us. He shook me hand as if I were a boy and called me Harry. He said something about me father. It were obvious he had known him. Captain Lee had a grey beard and kindly eyes. Ernie told me to look at Mount Wellington and tell me what I seen. I told him I seen a stick with a piece of cloth on it on its very top. The captain were impressed cos me eyes were sharper, sharper he said than any eyes he knew. Mr Carsons led me up the gangplank onto the deck while the crew were hurrying back and forth loading the ship. *Home,* he said to me, *This is your home now.*

When I said, *Me father? Becky?* he said aye, that if I stayed on the ship I would find them both. I took his words for the truth. He ordered me to climb up the rigging to the topmast and onto the crow's nest. I were nimble like a native cat, I have to say. I crawled up the rigging and then on to a spot on the topgallant crosstrees. They seen I had a head for heights and me sharp eyes could see for miles past Hobart town, past the harbour into the haze of the horizon a long way away. Down below the three men staring up at me were just specks like three flies stuck to sticky paper, and I knew, as if my father were whispering in me heart, that this spot up in the clouds were to be part of me job. It were me keen eyes that Captain Lee wanted.

When I returned to the deck, Captain Lee and Ernie and Mr Carsons were grinning. I pointed to the sea and asked as best I could where Becky and me father were and Captain Lee said aye, they were out there and I would find them after a long time. I had no idea of what a long time meant so I were happy to hear it. Mr Carsons and Ernie shook me hand and left the ship.

We set sail a few hours later. Captain Lee had me sleep in his cabin on the floor under his desk. He showed me pictures of whales and told me what to do if I seen one. He said I were never to eat with the crew but only with him. He told me to shit and piss in the early hours of the morning when there were hardly any crew on deck. He were real fond of maps and liked to show them to me. He pointed out where the ship had been before and where there could be whales. He had me learn the names of oceans and islands we were going to next.

The first few weeks the ship were bouncing, tossing, turning, rolling, jumping through wild waves and freezing wind that were like nails spearing me face. It were not til we were moving north into the Pacific that the seas calmed and the days grew warmer. Now I could spend me days aloft. I knew I were supposed to be gazing for whales, but after a time on the top of the ship you feel awfully distant from those ants below on the deck, and you dream. I dreamed of finding me father, maybe in one of those countries or islands I seen in Captain's Lee's atlas. Captain Lee always sent me up a few hours before dawn cos he knew I could see far in piccaninny light. I watched twice a day, before dawn and into the early hours of sunlight, and an hour or two before dusk when me eyes could see further than any other whale-spotter. I took a speaking trumpet with me cos me voice were light compared to the others on whale watch. So there I were, on top of the ship like a spider in the centre of a giant web of ropes, searching, searching, searching the horizon for a spout, ever so faint. Just a tiny puff and I knew what to yell out. Sometimes it were hard not to drift off in me head. The seas seem without end, the horizon is always the horizon and you never get to it, the ship rolling from side to side like a rocking chair putting me in some sort of trance, and I were not alone, behind me were another crewman on look-out duties and he – whoever he were, cos the men could only stand the job for two hours at a time – would be in a trance too and sometimes on sultry days when we were hardly moving, the ship swayed like a pendulum but it were as if time stood still. The regular rocking rhythm put we watchers on the main and mizzen mastheads into a daze where time, place and even our bodies did not exist.

When I looked behind me I seen a wake of water at the stern of the ship and I'd watch the wake slowly vanish, and it seemed to me our ship left no mark on the sea and even our ship did not exist. I began to see the ocean had many colours from bright emerald to a dirty grey. I'd stare at the quivering water, seeing that just beneath the surface it were shivering with life, teeming with the shadows and silhouettes of fish, the fish only becoming real when they jumped out of the sea into the air and flew for a few moments or the triangle fin of a shark or dolphin cut the surface. Then there were the times just after dusk or before dawn when the sea squirmed with dots of bright lights, like thousands of tiny lamps.

Other times I felt as if I were no longer attached to the ship, but like a sea eagle drifting in an air current, unattached to the earth and sea, carefree and happy as I daydreamed 'bout Becky and me father. Oh, it's hard to remember exactly what these fancies were. I suppose if I whacked me noggin a few times I might remember in detail, but it were so many years ago that it's vague, like seeing a thing slowly emerge from a sea fog or mist and you don't know if it's a whale, a demon or a ship til it's practically within touching distance. For some reason I got it into me noggin that Becky were waiting for me on some other ship and that she had been taken on board like me. When I seen a ship passing close by or anchored in a harbour I'd rush up to me possie and I'd be looking down on the deck of the other ship, trying to spot her. I had to cling to this dream just as me mind were clinging to the thought that me father had sailed down the Munro river out to sea and landed on some tropical island. You know,

I seen a magician once and he put a dog in a box and when he opened the box the dog was gone. But then it barked and you know what? It were now sitting on a woman's lap in the audience. That's the only way to describe it. I were waiting for Becky and me father to appear elsewhere, somewhere, cos even a dog could appear after disappearing.

Whales were hard to find, that much were clear. We had been sailing for two or three months and the sea were empty of them. We seen dolphins, sharks, flying fish and stingrays. We seen natives in canoes, and whaling ships returning to the United States full as a goog with sperm oil – they were easy to spot at night cos they used the whale oil for their lamps and torches. We seen them pass glittering like fairy lights in the night. Captain Lee hated those ships cos he said they were skiting with all their lamps and were trying to make whalers like us seem like failures. He used to grumble and turn away from the cabin window when he seen such braggart whalers. I knew to say nothing while he'd sit in his chair, sighing and lost in thought. Sometimes he'd talk to me, not wanting me to talk back, you know, how you talk to a dog. He were in pain. I had seen that stare on a man before. It were the look of Mr Carsons when he despaired of me and Becky becoming human again.

I kept me distance from the other crew and cos I slept in the Captain's quarters they knew I were under his protection. It were a crew of men from across the world: Australians, Maoris, Hawaiians, Americans, English, Poles, you name it. They'd sing when drunk and I'd hear their voices echoing through the whole ship as they sang of women, drinking and longing for home, whatever home they came from. I'd sit on deck and watch the crew show off their tattoos, some with pictures of naked women or anchors or dragons or hearts with arrows through them. Captain Lee asked Specky his cabin boy to teach me to talk proper. Specky was short for speck, Flyspeck – he were small. Like me he couldn't write or read but he would take me round, inside, on top of the ship, teaching me the names of objects. Sometimes I looked down from me possie on the topgallant and seen him grabbing some fellow and pointing up at me in me heavenly nest and laugh, like he thought I were funny and he'd twirl his finger round the side of his head and laugh again. I knew he were poking fun at me and sometimes I thought of whacking him just at the memory of him taking the mickey out of me. It would be easy cos he were 'bout my height and skinny like he were a skeleton with only a paper-thin skin wrapped round his bones. Once when we were anchored near an island the crew undressed Specky and threw him into the lagoon cos he were so on the nose. I swear that when they dragged him back onto the ship and he flopped on the deck gasping for air that I could see his heart beating, like he were one of those geckos whose heart you can see under their thin pale skin. I felt sorry for him then – I knew what it were like not to be seen as human.

But he could be a pest, that Specky. One day he found me below deck getting a pineapple for

Captain Lee. He came up behind me, held me tightly and said he wanted to play a game. He threw himself on me, kissing me roughly. The pineapple was still in my hand so I smashed it on his head. He fell to his knees and passed out, his face and hair splattered with pineapple gunk and juice. The rest of the crew called me *Little Man Harry* and would make jokes 'bout me and Captain Lee I didn't understand but cos I were the best whale-spotter by far they knew they had to treat me good or I would tell the Captain.

Captain Lee drank by himself. When he were in a good mood he would talk and talk to me, not expecting an answer but telling me of times, years before, when the oceans were filled with whales and fortunes were made just from one voyage. The best times were when he spoke about me father and how he were a great whaler with a dead-eye-dick aim with the lance. There were one time when me father got tangled up with the rope attached to the lance and he found himself being whipped out of the boat and for a few terrible moments he were pinned to the whale's back as it were frothing in agony before submerging. He only survived cos he had a knife and cut himself free of the rope just as the whale dived down into the deep. When he had drunk too much Captain Lee would fall into a black mood and tell himself why did he bother any more and what were the point – the oceans were huge, the number of whales tiny. He said it were like looking for a diamond in seven seas of shit.

One morning I woke up and seen Captain Lee, not in his bed, but curled up in the corner of the cabin covered in his own vomit. He were so still I thought for a moment he were dead but he were snoring softly, the empty whiskey bottle rolling back and forth across the cabin floor. It were two hours before dawn and, after filling me pockets with bread, I grabbed me trumpet and inched me way up into the sky.

It were near dawn and the sun were creeping up from the grey sea when the first rays spread over the water and me heart suddenly went ping! A few miles ahead I thought I seen the black hull of an overturned boat. I peered closer and seen it were moving. I knew what that meant. I were so excited that instead of shouting out I found meself making warning coughs. Then I seen the trumpet in me hand and I yelled into it, *There she blows!* There were only a couple of blokes on the deck. They looked up at me. I pointed and shouted down at them again: *There she blows!* In a blink, men poured out from below deck, running, shouting, stumbling. *Where away?* I heard Captain Lee call out to me. I pointed ahead of me just as another tiny puff rose up from the whale. *How far?* he cried out. Captain Lee looked through his telescope at where I were pointing. He started to bark orders, *Calling all hands! Get the boats ready.* Even now I can hear me excited voice – *There she blows!* – really loud, really shrill, so shrill it cut the muggy air so everybody below heard it.

Captain Lee ordered the helmsman to keep the ship steady in the direction I were pointing out. *Can you make out more than one whale?* Captain Lee shouted.

I seen the flukes of two other whales near the first one. The ship bore down on the whales. Me body were tingling and me heart were beating fast like I were back with the tigers hunting down our prey. The chase had begun.

As we neared the beasts I counted five of them. Cap-tain Lee's were the only voice coming from the deck as he shouted his orders, *Keep her steady! Steady at the helm! There steady . . . 'bout half a mile off.* Then he went silent. I could feel the excitement and keenness of the crew as they stared at the giants just ahead. Captain Lee cried out, *Hoist and swing the boats!* Three boats were lowered into the water and the men rowed silently, creeping up on their prey. Captain Lee were in the first boat. As he neared the whales, they saw him, snorted loudly, slapped the sea with their flukes and dived. The crews stopped rowing and waited for the whales to reappear. Captain Lee smoked his pipe and watched the water for half an hour, then there were a ripple of white water, a loud sighing, whistling spouts, the air trembling, the water troubled. There were a hollow roar and a black mass rushed up only a few yards from Captain Lee's boat, bouncing it like it were a bath toy. The whale were 'bout twice the size of the boat, maybe more. I seen the barnacles and white blotches of sea lice on its skin. Captain Lee jumped up after tumbling down and aimed the harpoon. He threw it and it sunk deep into the creature's back. The whale dived again and cos the lance were attached to a rope it towed the Captain's boat over the horizon and out of sight. We set off after it.

By the time we caught up with the boat the poor monster were rolling, tumbling in a flurry of its own blood. It seemed mad with pain and its flukes lashed out at the boat, as if trying to smash it. Its spout hole were opening and closing til finally there were a rush and gush of clotted red blood that shot into the air – like its heart had burst.

It took hours to tie the dead animal up to the side of the ship, which groaned at the weight of the beast. Sharks attacked the whale and the men standing on the monster's back drove their whale spades deep into the shark skulls. There were gore, blood and frenzy as sharks turned on their own kind, and tore out the intestines, livers and stomachs of each other while the seabirds screamed overhead as if they too were crazed by the killing and gore. The thick blubber were cut off in long strips like peeling an orange. There were men, blubber, gunk, blood and grease sloshing back and forth cross the deck. There were constant shouting and men sliding across the deck like they were skating across the blood and muck. The cutters tried to stay perched on the whale's slippery back as it hanged on the side of the ship while they hacked into the blubber and all the time keeping an eye on the ferocious sharks foaming up the sea and snapping at the whalers just a few feet away.

Two great try-pots were set up on the deck as twilight came and with it the cry of *Fire the works!* The bowls became two furnaces and by the time it were night they were aflame as the crew throwed the chunks of blubber into the burning pots, the blubber burning with a hiss as if the whale were protesting his death piece by piece. Soot and smoke rolled across the decks and out onto the ocean. Everyone were sweaty and black with soot. The smoke burned our throats. The hunks of blubber were boiled down into oil and poured into casks. The din of the hissing, shouting, laughing and yelling were deafening. Far into the night the spouts of flames soared up into the yardarms, warming me into the very marrow of me bones. More blubber were chucked into the fire and the whole ship were hazy with clouds of greasy black smoke. The men's faces and clothes were coated in soot, smoke, grease and blood and they stinked of cooked blubber. They looked like they were savages or demons dancing round two sacrifices. From me eyrie up top, the burning pots looked like two demon's eyes. Even with the bloody horror, the smell and the rancid smoke, I were happy cos we had finally made a killing.

I were watching all this when I seen a bloodied crew-man hand Captain Lee something he had found in the whale. It were about the size of a football. He smelt it. I knew immediately what it were and I scrambled down the rigging as fast as possible. By the time I were on deck Captain Lee had gone to his cabin. I rushed there only to see him come out, closing the door behind him. When he seen me he smiled and tapped me on the shoulder. *Good work, Harry*, he said and went back up on deck. I made sure no one were watching and I crept into the cabin and seen what I were after on his desk. It were ambergris. I sniffed it. It smelt both of stink and something spicy and sweet. I knew I were stealing, but I didn't care. I ripped off a piece about the size of an egg and returned to my possie on top of the mast. There, while the men toiled below me, I slowly chewed a small piece of the ambergris; it were awfully smelly but underneath that stink I smelt the scent of flowers.

And as I nibbled at it the past came back to me – a storm of memories, good and bad. There were Mr Carsons telling me that me mother and me father were dead. And in remembering that terrible moment – like me flesh were pierced with the lance of truth – I knew that I would not find me father. He were dead. He were a ghost. But all the smells, the whale, the try-works – it all seemed to be saying to me that me father's ghost were part of the ship. When I thought that his ghost were part of the ship it became a big comfort to me. There were other memories: me, me mother and father and Becky in the boat on the Munro river, the picnic and almost drowning. But there were also good stuff of Becky and me and the tigers, hunting down prey, running barefoot through the snow, sleeping together, lazing in the sun, tasting fresh blood and Becky and me, like two kids in a fairytale, following the tigers to their den and safety. And us on the beach, our minds tingling as we ate the ambergris, our flesh alive as it could ever be. And then, one memory came back that still stanged me like the first time – Becky turning round in the gig to wave goodbye to me as she headed off into the mist, leaving me in that Hobart hotel room. Maybe the ambergris made me giddy, but up there above the smoking, fiery deck I felt closer to the heavens, closer to her, almost as if she were beside me, inside me, and she thinking of me at that moment. And I had this feeling deep in me that we were bound together forever and I would see her again.

I only ate a bit of the ambergris and hid the rest

in a tobacco tin, knowing Becky would like it and I'd give it to her once I tracked her down.

I were good at me job and we killed several more whales. When we were returning to Hobart I seen one of the Maori crew tattooing his mates. He were real good at it, and at scrimshawing too. I asked him if he would tattoo me. He laughed and said that I were just a kid and I'd cry if he cut me skin. I said I wouldn't and I didn't. How I put up with the pain is a mystery but I were determined to show them I were a man. He gave me a piece of bone to bite on, which were just as well as I were in lots of pain. But I weren't going to show it. I were so proud when he finished. My arm were sore but the crew knew I were no coward. Me tattoo may be a little fainter now but you can easily see her name – *Becky*. Later I were pissed off when I found out the mistake the Maori made but I got to laugh. I didn't know how to spell and the Maori didn't either. What can I do?

B E K C Y is there on my left arm til I kick the bucket. I knew it said Becky, though, no matter it were the wrong spelling.

When we were heading back home I were glad. P'raps I could find her back in Hobart. We docked one summer morning. I don't know what I expected. I s'pose I thought Becky would be waiting for me. But there were only the wives and friends of the crew. No Becky. No Mr Carsons. I were sorely down in the dumps when I seen a sulky arrive and in it were Ernie, plump as a cow bloated with cloverleaf. He waved to me. I were happy to see someone I knew. I ran down the gangplank and into his warm arms. He hugged me and then stepped back to examine me. *Hannah, how you've grown*, he said. He told me that Mr Carsons couldn't come cos it were sheep-shearing time. He asked me some questions but I only had one thing on me mind and I asked him where Becky were. He frowned, which threw me. Why were he frowning? Was something wrong? *You will hear her when we're back at my place*, he said.

Ernie had a long meeting with Captain Lee while I waited in the sulky, jiggling with impatience, for I had got it in me silly young mind that Becky were at Ernie's house. I thought it were going to be a surprise. It didn't take us long to get to Battery Point where Ernie lived. When he pointed out his house I jumped from the sulky and ran up to the door and tried to get in. But it were locked. I knocked and knocked and called Becky's name til Ernie arrived, panting with effort as usual, to open the door for me.

I ran inside, whirling in and out of rooms, but she were not there. I kept on asking where she were. Ernie put his finger to his lips to shhhh me and told me to follow him. He went to the end of the corridor, and opened a narrow side door. Me heart were pounding in excitement at the thought of seeing Becky. I followed Ernie down the stairs into the basement. At the bottom of the stairs he turned on a switch. Dozens of globes lit up, like it had become high noon, it were that bright, but what astonished me were all the machines and technical equipment he had: wiring, screws, bells, saws, piping, copper plates, cylinders of all sizes, metal boxes. I were stunned by all these strange objects, but I also had Becky on my mind and she didn't seem to be in the basement. I were looking under a table in case she were hiding when Ernie led me to a bench. I recognised the machine. It were like the one at Mr Carsons's farm. He turned a tiny brass handle and placed a needle on the hollow black cylinder. There was the sound of a girl's voice, as if she were singing from a faraway room. It were Becky's voice and she were singing a song without words I had never heard before. It were a simple tune but sung in a throaty way, where you make more than one pitch at a time. It sounded ancient like a dark green forest full of tree ferns at twilight, their fronds catching the last rays of the pale sun.

Me heart beat fast, and me mind were filled with the ecstasy of hearing her. I knew she were singing to me. *Where is she?* I kept on asking, but all Ernie would say were that Becky were far away. Where were far away? I asked but Ernie just shrugged and said it were a long way away. He explained that Becky had made the recording just for me. There were no need for him to tell me that; I knew it. I knew by the beautiful tune that she were saying to me, *I still think of you. You are not my friend, you are my sister. We have an unbreakable bond forever.*

I were so excited I asked Ernie to play it again and again til he said if I played it any more the song would vanish. He asked me if I would like to send her a song. Would I? Course I would. Ernie took me outside where he set up a recording machine with an enormous horn about the length of a man and which I were to sing into while the needle put me song into the wax cylinder. But what would I sing? The only song I knew all the way through were one that I heard on the whaler. The crew sang it when they were working round the windlass and capstan. It were called 'Hurrah, my boys, we're homeward bound'. The last bit went: '*We're homeward bound,*' *you've heard us say, 'Goodbye, fare-ye-well, Goodbye, fare-ye-well.' Hook on the cat then, and rut her away.*

Ernie played it back to me. I didn't recognise me voice. It sounded like a boy's. There were also the sounds of the crickets and birds when I were singing. Ernie said he would send it to Becky so she could hear me and know I were thinking of her. It were then I remembered what I had in me bag. I ran up the stairs and returned with a handkerchief tied in a knot. I undid it and showed Ernie the last bit of the ambergris, about the size of a marble. I told him to give it to Becky when he gave her my song. He promised he would.

The days were long while I waited for an answer. There were nothing for me to do. I watched Ernie build his phonographs and telephones. His fingers were chubby but he were so delicate when he worked, even fixing the tiniest parts of a machine. It seemed a miracle to me the way he put everything together to become a phonograph or telephone. To test the telephone he asked me to go upstairs where he had set up a receiver. He told me to answer it when he rang from his phone in the basement. I jumped when the bell rang and when I picked it up and put the tiny trumpet against me ear I heard nothing except a faint grumbling noise, like it were the sea. Then I heard Ernie's voice saying hello, like he were next to me. I jumped in surprise. It seemed a miracle that his voice would go all through the wires and pop out of the hearing horn. Now, of course, people take telephones and record players for granted; but Ernie, who were an inventor and obsessed by voices one might say, whether it be on a wax cylinder or coming through the telephone wires, were one of the few people in Hobart who knew anything about these novelties, for that's what they were at that time.

If he didn't need me he became so caught up in his work he hardly knew I were there, if at all, so I'd go out into the back yard and lie under the apple and almond trees looking at the sky, daydreaming and growing bored. I were used to doing things. I didn't like doing too much thinking cos I ended up feeling low 'bout me mother and father drowning and Becky being so far from me. Some times as I lied in the long grass I'd find meself remembering Dave and Corinna and in remembering I thought that those times were a kind of paradise. I know we were cold and hungry sometimes but mostly it were good times. I liked Ernie, but I liked whaling better. Hunting agreed with me. I liked feeling the sudden pumping of me blood when I seen a whale and the cry of *Lower the boat!* as the ship moved in on a monster.

In the evenings Ernie and I walked down to the harbour. He called me Harry cos I were still pretending to be a boy. When I seen girls my age I were puzzled as to how fragile they seemed in their pretty dresses and long curly hair. Their lives were not for me. Ernie didn't cook much and we ate at one of the seamen's hotels. He ate huge til he would go puce in the face and burp a lot, especially when he'd had a few beers.

When we were eating he'd sometimes smile at me, shake his head and say, *To think I met you cos of my machines.* And he tell me the story of how he came to find us. He were travelling through the bush with his phonograph recording the songs of farmers, shepherds, drunks and old women. He thought these songs would soon die out and be forgotten and believed it were his mission to make sure this didn't happen. He were coming from a bounty hunter's place when he heard a man call out to him. The man had a long black, unruly beard and were starvation thin. His eyes were feverish with purpose and he looked as ancient as any prophet in the Old Testament. He told Ernie that he had been searching for two girls for four years, only stopping for winter and the lambing season. He asked if Ernie had seen or heard about the girls. The strange thing is that he had. The bounty hunter were a half breed and were one of the last who could sing blackfella songs. When Ernie had finished recording him the blackfella told him a story about how he had seen two girls hunting with tigers. Ernie thought the story were a fib or myth. When Ernie told Mr Carsons about the blackfella's story Mr Carsons demanded to talk to him, so they returned to the bounty hunter and he told Mr Carsons where he had seen the girls and where he suspected they had a lair. Ernie were curious if this were true and he asked to come with Mr Carsons in the search for us. Five days later they spotted us through binoculars. We were naked, scrawny, covered in dirt and moss and with long matted hair, and walked with a strange animal-like gait or on all fours. *You didn't look like two girls but a nightmare version of them*, he'd say, then he'd let his jaw drop and his eyes pop open in astonishment, as if he were seeing us that first time. He looked so funny that we'd laugh and laugh and meat spitted out of his mouth and down his green vest. He were like me – he hated vegetables and he'd say to the cook when he ever attempted to put even a potato on Ernie's plate, *I am an animal. All humans are animals and if it's good enough for animals only to eat meat, then it's good enough for me.*

One night as we were polishing off our meals I overheard a couple of blokes talking about a whaler 'bout to set off on a voyage in two days' time. The news stayed with me and when Ernie and I were making our way back to his old house on the hill I stopped to look back at the whaler. It were blazing with lights as the crew hurried to finish restocking. I looked up at the top of the mainmast where I imagined meself sitting, keeping an eager eye out for any signs of whales. Then I seen Captain Lee come on deck. I ran down to the water's edge and called out to him. He seen me and waved back. Ernie and I joined him on the ship. Captain Lee were like me, he had no family in Hobart and he were bored too. He had hired a new crew and were keen to have me on the voyage. I were the best spotter he had ever had.

Ernie could tell I were very excited to be returning to the sea. The strange thing about ships is despite them being crowded and stinky and at the mercy of

Nature, most times they are like wooden islands of freedom, free from petty concerns and the laws of the land. All we did were hunt and if we were not hunting we were preparing to do so. There seemed a purpose that I didn't find on land. Perhaps it were also me father's spirit that were snuggled inside me.

After agreeing I would return to whaling with Captain Lee, Ernie helped me pack and took me down to the docks. He said he would see me off the following morning. I put me trunk into me spot in the corner of Captain Lee's cabin then crawled up the rigging to me possie and sat there rocking softly as the strong tide came up through the Derwent River. You could call that small wooden seat me home, if I had a home. Next morning as we prepared to set out I seen Ernie arrive and slowly, with puffing effort, get out of his gig like a slug leaving behind its shell. He waved to me to come and say goodbye. I clambered down the rigging and were heading to the gangplank when I seen a lean, bearded figure gallop up on a piebald horse.

It were Mr Carsons. He began talking ten to the dozen into Ernie's ear. Ernie shook his head once or twice and then nodded a lot til finally the two motioned me to come and talk to them. I ran down the gangplank. I were awfully glad to see Becky's father cos I thought he were there to take me to her. I were asking him to take me to her when he suddenly shouted at me to shut up. He looked stern and his eyes were cold and bright like someone 'bout to throw a harpoon into a whale's side. *Now, listen to me*, he said, grabbing both me arms and squeezing them and covering me face and his beard in spittle, *We have a big adventure for you. You are going to find Rebecca.* I didn't quite understand and Ernie repeated what Becky's father had said.

Captain Lee were sad to see me go. It were only when we were at the stables packing the horses with food, camping equipment, ropes and rifles that I realised we were going on a long journey and something inside me made me heart beat fast like when I were afeared in the bush and I sensed danger. From what I could understand – and let me tell you, Mr Carsons were a man of very few words – Becky were lost somewhere and we were off to go searching for her. I were told she were far away. A fear gripped me – were they going to take me far, far away so that I would not be heard of again like her? I told them I had sanged to her but she hadn't come. They asked me again to come with them. I shook me head like it were going to fall off. I felt dread in the pit of me stomach. I wanted to return to the ship and Captain Lee. The ship would help me find her, not Mr Carsons, who seemed loony. His eyes were shiny with a mad purpose. I said I weren't going and I were going back to Captain Lee cos I didn't believe they were going to find her and how come they lost her?

I started to walk back to the ship, Ernie told me to stop. *Sing to her this time,* he said, *and she will come back to you.* I were unsure, but I trusted Ernie. He sat me down on a bale of hay and said, *I will tell you the truth about us and your Becky.* Mr Carsons stood against the wall of the stables puffing on his pipe, leaving Ernie to tell me the truth.

Ernie told me he knew what Becky had gone through cos he and Becky used to spend time together and yabber a lot. Then he flabbergasted me by saying that the real reason why Becky were far away were cos of the ambergris I gave him to pass on to her.

He said that, like me, Becky thought every day of that morning in Hobart when we were separated. As she were driven away in the buggy she looked back and seen me staring out the window and in her heart she felt something awful was going to happen to the both of us. She had a slimy feeling in the pit of her stomach that we were going to be separated for a long time.

Mr Carsons had decided to tear us apart. He thought that Becky and I were not good for each other, that we were not learning what we should and our bond meant that I were holding Becky back. That misty morning Becky were taken to a boarding school where the headmistress, Miss Davis, were told that Becky had been schooled on the farm and it were now time she were taught properly. Mr Carsons and Ernie told Becky that I were being sent to a school on the mainland to get special education cos I were more backward than she were.

Becky were sent to a Church of England school for girls. It's still there. It were once on the outskirts of Hobart almost swallowed up by the bush. Over the years the city has surrounded it so that its gardens have shrunk and the bush gone. I visited it once, years after Becky went there. It's built of sandstone and has narrow windows that makes it seem like a gaol. I stood at the closed iron gates and tried to imagine just how Becky were feeling as she were driven up the long driveway to the main house. She had been taken from me and now she were to live and learn at the school. Mr Carsons thought that she needed to be with girls her own age and teachers who would educate her properly. After warning Becky that she must never tell anyone 'bout me and her living with the tigers, Mr Carsons went back to his farm. The only person she knew in Hobart were Ernie, who would visit her every weekend. He knew she'd be lonely cos all the other girls had visitors or went home for the weekend.

It were hard for her to fit in. She slept in a dormitory with the other girls. They teased her cos of the way she'd sniff them or the funny way she spoke. For the first few months she found it difficult to sleep at night. She'd sit for hours in her bed looking out the window, watching the night animals move across the school gardens. If she didn't do that she'd get up and walk through the dormitory watching the girls sleep and wondering why they didn't like her. One day it occurred to her that she had to find a way of fitting in and the way to do it were to mimic the other girls. She'd copy a girl's way of talking, someone's way of making hand movements and someone's way of walking. When she began to walk with a limp the poor girl she were copying thought she were being teased and attacked Becky, who on being hit jumped on the girl, tearing at her hair and biting her arm. It took several teachers to pull her off. The headmistress wanted to get rid of Becky but Ernie promised she would behave. Becky told Ernie why she were copying the girl with a limp – cos she wanted to walk like the other girls and be thought of as one of them. He told her to copy a normal student's walk. He were good for her, that Ernie.

Sometimes he'd take her to his house and record her singing on the phonograph. But he kept lying to her. Every weekend she'd ask Ernie where I were, what I were doing and when we'd see each other again. He told her that I were enjoying me own learning at a special school far away and that he were sending her phonograph songs to me. He also said that we would see each other soon. Soon! It were always soon! But it never happened.

After the incident with the limping girl, Miss Davis and Ernie tried to find different ways for Becky to mix with the other students and become more normal, I s'pose. Her English were really going great guns, but she were still awkward round other girls and they didn't like the way she'd stare at them with what they said were *a strange look*. I know what they meant. People still say that 'bout me. When I go to the local store the shopkeeper, Mr Dixon, says I stare at him as if he were food. But it's not that. It's not even that I'm listening to his words. What I am doing is closely watching his body and his eyes to see what he's thinking of doing next or what he's actually thinking. It's what me and Becky learned when we were with the tigers. It's the body and eyes that tell what a person is thinking or going to do. That's why I stare at people down the village or on the track when I run into them. I can tell when they're interested in what I'm saying or when they're curious or when they're nervous. Mr Dixon said me gaze were putting off his customers so he gave me a pair of sunglasses to wear when I visit his shop. Even years after me and Becky were with Dave and Corinna, this ability or curse, name it what you will, were still there.

One day Miss Davis seen Becky with the gardener's hound. It were a big dog and all the girls were scared of it but in Becky the dog recognised a kindred spirit and one where she were its master. The girls and Miss Davis were amazed at how the dog would roll over on its back and expose its belly to Becky. One day as she were nuzzling the dog Miss Davis asked Becky a question that had obviously been on her mind for some time. *Who are you, Rebecca?*

I am Becky, she replied. *Why are you like this?* asked the headmistress. Becky didn't understand the question. Then Miss Davis said – and Becky told Ernie she found this a very difficult order to understand or even obey – *You are not to go near this dog again.* Those words stanged Becky. She said the dog were her friend. Miss Davis told Ernie that Becky must mix with the other girls, other people, rather than dogs – and there were a solution. She said that Becky must perform in the school play, which they did every year with the boys from a school down the road.

She were told to act in one of several little plays based on fairy stories. The teacher who were doing the plays got Becky to play Little Red Riding Hood. It were hard for her to work out how to pretend. She could easily remember the lines, *Easy as pie*, she said to Ernie when he asked her how she were handling it. The problem were that it were difficult for her to know exactly what were going on. One girl were pretending to be a grandma and a boy were pretending to be a wolf. This were truly hard for Becky to figure out. Plainly the boy were not a wolf. He didn't even act like a real one. It were easy for Becky not to be afeared of him cos he were so not like a wolf or dog but what puzzled her were how the boy became a wolf and a grandma at the same time. And when Becky said, *Oh Grandma, what big eyes you've got*, she could not understand why she were saying it cos the boy had tiny eyes, nothing like a tiger's eyes, for instance. Other things confused her. During rehearsal she had to pretend she had food in her basket but there were no food in it. The teacher kept on saying that she had to *pretend*. That didn't work. It were only when she said it were a game that Becky sort of got the hang of it.

It were a couple of days before the performance when Ernie told Becky an audience were coming to watch the plays. She became excited by that cos she were hankering after her father and Ernie said he would be there. The theatre night were held one spring evening on the school lawns. The parents and visitors were seated at long tables lit by hundreds of candles. A stage were built on the lawns. There were three plays, one about Cinderella, one 'bout the Pied Piper of Hamelin and Becky's play which were to come between the other two cos they had more actors in them, especially the Pied Piper which had dozens of girls from the lower forms who were playing the rats.

After Becky got dressed in her red dress, cloak and hood, Ernie took her aside and explained that her father would not be able to get to see the show in time cos he were marooned inland due to a flood.

As a gift to ease her disappointment Ernie gave her me ambergris. She were over the moon. It meant everything to her cos it came from me. She were so thrilled cos she thought I were going to see the show too. Ernie had to tell her I were not going to be there. *Why can't Hannah and I see each other?* she pleaded. Ernie said she'd soon find out. But when were soon?

Ernie sat down with the rest of the audience, which were a considerable size cos the parents were from both the boys' and girls' schools. While the Cinderella story were on stage Becky didn't watch it cos she were so caught up in smelling the ambergris. It brought back memories of me and Dave and Corinna. It were as powerful on her as it were on me. Then she did something that Ernie were to regret. As she waited to go on stage he saw her eat the ambergris. It didn't take long before her face were filled with bliss. I knew the feeling; all her senses were alight and alive and sparkling with the rush of memories.

She were so caught up in her bliss that one of the teachers had to push her on stage. When she were up there she stopped, rooted to the spot. She seen all those people sitting at the tables – and it striked her that they were staring at her, which made her very nervous, so much so that she forgot her lines. The boy who were dressed up as a wolf came towards her. She tensed, placed all her attention on him, and lost any sense that she were on stage in front of an audience. It were like she were really in the woods and she were not afeared of the big bad wolf. In fact, she laughed. Her blood were now hot and pulsating and forgetting where she were, she moved in on the boy like he were the prey rather than the other way round. His tiny eyes were firefly-bright with fear and he moved away but she circled him, waiting for the wolf to make his break when she would pounce. She could smell his fear – and that only made her even more thrilled. *Stay away! Stay away!* the boy were yelling. Becky stopped for a moment cos she heard some of the audience laugh and she were annoyed cos she were serious and she gave them a threat yawn which silenced them. Then she went back to herding the boy into a corner. A teacher must have realised something were wrong cos she rushed on the stage and grabbed Becky, who turned on her growling and giving the threat yawn. The boy ran off the stage and Becky yanked herself free to give chase. She ran through the dozens of girls dressed as rats. They all screamed and ran away but Becky only had eyes for the boy. In her mind she were now hunting prey.

The boy ran down the lawns to the tables crying out for his mother and father. Teachers tried to stop Becky but she snarled and spit at them and chased the boy round a long table. There were so much panic that people knocked over the candles. Soon the tablecloths were on fire. There were screaming and shrieking and crying. But Becky were laughing cos she were having the time of her life. As she continued after the crying boy she suddenly seen Ernie coming towards her. He lunged at her but she easily jumped out of his way and then she was off. She ran through the screaming, burning mayhem and the squealing, panic-stricken rats and raced through the gardens out to the back of the school into the bushland, never looking back. She ran and ran and ran and vanished into the night.

We think we know where she's gone and we think we know what she's looking for, Hannah, said Ernie finishing his story and getting up from the bale of hay he had been sitting on. He motioned to his packhorse near the stable door. I recognised one of his phonographs with a huge speaking horn strapped to its side. *Do you believe me now?* he asked. I looked at his gentle face and then at Mr Carsons hitting his pipe against the wall. He looked tormented and I knew I had been told the truth and we were truly going to search for her.

Mr Carsons were in a hurry and we set off right away in a drizzling mist, through the streets of Hobart and out of the city. Mr Carsons didn't give me a horse so I rode with Ernie. During the rough sections of the bush I'd try to wrap me arms round his stomach, which were so fat me fingers couldn't meet, so I put me hands into his jacket pockets. That first night, after we had made camp and eaten, Mr Carsons tied me to Ernie's leg so I wouldn't run away, which were stupid cos I had no idea where Becky were and I needed the men to help me. Ernie had a flask of whiskey and as he sipped it he stared at the flames like someone looking at tea-leaves trying to see the future. I listened to the night birds and animals hunting for food, snuffling, grunting, snarling, crunching bones, crackling dead leaves. It were like I were coming home. I knew what the sounds meant. I could see in me mind what the devils, possums and owls were doing. I thought I heard the cough of a tiger and I spun round in the direction of the sound when Ernie leaned over and touched me hand, tapping it like he were doing Morse code of apology, saying to me how sorry he were to take me on this trip. I said I were fine with it cos we were going to find lost Becky. He asked me how might Becky survive. I said most likely she'd eat berries, catch creek crayfish and baby animals. *It might take a long while*, he said, glancing across at Mr Carsons sleeping in his bag. *It took years to find you and Rebecca in the bush. Everyone else gave up, but not Mr Carsons.*

Next morning as we followed the river Mr Carsons asked me if I recognised the place where Becky and me had nearly drowned. I shook me head cos it were all vague to me til one day, just before we stopped for lunch, I felt the slam of memory hit me. There it were – the bend in the river, the bank where we were saved by the tiger and, lo and behold, in a tree were the remains of me father's boat.

Is this your father's boat? Mr Carsons asked me and at that moment I seen in me mind me father struggling under water and me mother gone. The sight of the boat told me like no words could that me mother and me father were now ghosts. I began to weep. Ernie hugged me til I were cried out but I noticed that Mr Carsons looked at me without a skerrick of pity or grief. He had the dead eyes of a harpooner aiming for the heart of a whale.

After we had eaten, Mr Carsons asked me which way Becky and I had gone with the tiger. I pointed the way into that forest and its trees so high that you'd strain your neck to see their tops which were a tangled darkness blotting out the sun, cloaked in moss and vines and giant tree ferns – it were a land for giants. It were obvious that Mr Carsons thought Becky in running away from the school had taken the path along the river and were following the trail we had taken those years before. Ernie suggested we take a short cut and make for the lair, which meant continuing straight upstream til we got to the clear country, but Mr Carsons were of the mind that his daughter might be starving and ill and unable to make her way to the lair and he didn't want to go the easy way just in case we accidentally bypassed her.

But we found no sign of her by the time we rode onto the tablelands. As he had done the previous three days, Mr Carsons woke up early and spent the hours before breakfast calling out Becky's name. He never got an answer except when it were an echo that seemed more desperate than the actual cry of her name. I knew he were hoping that his daughter were making for the lair, but had she made it that far? In the late afternoons when the air were still and crisp Ernie would unpack his phonograph and set it up in a clear space and he'd play the cylinder with me singing the sea shanty. He did not play it too often cos he said my voice and her voice would wear away til the songs were lost forever.

But something were happening to me that I only gradually noticed – I stayed awake most of the night, me hearing becoming real keen, me eyes sharper too. I heard the slightest rustle of animals looking for prey. I heard the squeal of animals being killed. The sounds of their struggle for life made me tingle with fear and excitement. I felt meself one with the night. I were reliving the thrill of setting out with Becky and the tigers on a hunt, the sense of the four of us being at one with our purpose and the sheer, juicy thrill of the chase, our thumping hearts, the way we each knew without words what to do, the tigers running ahead in a circle to turn back as Becky and I run after the quarry yelling and shouting and scaring the bejesus out of the prey who did not see the tigers waiting for them til the last moment when it were too late and the last thing the victim seen were the gleaming eyes and jaws that opened so wide that to the prey it must have seemed they would be swallowed whole. Oh, it felt good to see a fresh dead animal. We'd all be panting with effort and Becky and I would be smiling with pride cos we had helped in the kill. And then, I make no apology for this, there were the taste of the blood or bloody meat and it were like the first time I tasted seal gristle and my nerves tingled cos the blood and meat were so fresh that it were like we were tasting life even though the prey were just dead. And I knew that the owl felt the same thing after killing a mouse or quoll. I knew that the Tasmanian devils – which were easy to hear of a night cos of their spitting, hissing and snarling – didn't feel the joyful surge like us girls and the tigers, cos they ate putrid dead animals. That's why I didn't like the devils – they always feasted on death and didn't have the nous to hunt down prey like we did. I could smell when they were afeared cos they stink, but when they're not afeared they smell like lanolin. An animal afeared is a dreadful thing cos their whole body is scared, even their blood is afeared. Even now, I can't help it, but the squeals of an animal being killed is something that makes me blood run hot on hearing the sounds and me flesh shiver with anticipation. Me flesh wins over me heart.

There were something else going on in the night as we headed towards the lake and that were a different sound, like a heavy animal circling our camp, snapping twigs and heavy of footsteps. The first night I heard this creature I knew not what it were, but the second night, I thought it were Becky. Maybe it were, maybe it were not, but Mr Carsons woke and grabbed his rifle. He asked me if it were Becky that were making the noises. I said I didn't know. He asked if it were tigers. I said I didn't know cos the wind were blowing the wrong way and I couldn't smell them. Ernie were awake and he said something that stayed with me. He said to Mr Carsons, *Just what do you intend to do with Rebecca when you find her?* Mr Carsons did not answer. I noticed he had his finger on the trigger ready to shoot at a moment's notice.

By the time we were ready to ride out, a mist were moving through the ferns and trees like it were a creature smothering everything, so that we could barely see a couple of yards in front of us, but that didn't stop Mr Carsons, cos he were on his mission. It were the sort of mist that soaked into your flesh, into your being, so it were like you were one with it and it made me keenly aware of the smells of the earth, the ferns, flowers, shit, and all sounds were clear and sharp so I could not only hear the breathing of the horses but even feel the heartbeat of the horse I were on. In such a heavy mist you can hear a currawong stretch its wings and a rat scurry across damp leaves. I also smelt something the mist carried – a tiger's scent.

We rode closely together so we wouldn't lose each other and Mr Carsons must have noticed me sniffing the mist cos he asked what I were smelling. And I told him. I said I smelt a tiger, a female one. *We must be getting close*, he said and then fell into his dark silence again til in late afternoon when the mist drained away and birds began to cry and screech again and he got Ernie to set up the phonograph.

It were strange to hear me voice echoing through the valley and to hear me singing, *Hurrah, my boys, we're homeward bound. 'We're homeward bound,' you've heard us say, 'Goodbye, fare-ye-well, Goodbye, fare-ye-well.' Hook on the cat then, and rut her away.* I thought to meself – just what will Becky think when she hears it? Will she recognise me voice? Will she know it's me?

Mr Carsons were in a funny mood, funny peculiar, and he demanded Ernie play it again and again til Mr Carsons came to his senses when even he realised that the grooves in the wax cylinder were becoming smooth and me voice were draining away to nothing.

We were now heading straight for the den where the men had found Becky and me last time. We camped overnight and shivered in our tent as we tried to shelter from the freezing rain. In the morning it were really sunny and I had to squint cos the sun were reflecting off the wet, stony tablelands and almost blinding me. We didn't stop for lunch but rode on til we came to a clump of trees near the den. I were twitchy with expectations of seeing

Becky. And there were something else – I could smell a tiger nearby and it stank of Corinna.

Mr Carsons told Ernie and me to make sure we didn't make any noise. The phonograph was set up and the horn pointed to the entrance of the den. Before playing the song Mr Carsons did something that flooded me whole body with dread. He took off his neckerchief and tied it round me mouth. He looked at me with his burning eyes and told me not to say a thing. But the panic were pouring through me and me heart felt like it were going to burst through me ribs. I were afeared he were going to do something awful to Becky. I struggled and tried to bite through the neckerchief. Mr Carsons ordered Ernie to whack me if I tried to yell or give away our position.

Ernie played me song and it echoed through the trees and across the creek bed to where the den were, while Mr Carsons, rifle ready, stood stock-still rooted to the ground like an ancient tree. If I didn't know before, it were deadly certain now why the two men had taken me there – Mr Carsons were afeared that Becky might keep running away if it were only him and Ernie. I were there, well, me voice were anyway, to entice Becky to come back with us. Me voice were to be used to call her, to sing her home.

Sure enough me heart went thump and me breath stopped as if I were in a spell when I seen Becky slowly emerge from the den and stand up and look round, amazed at hearing the song. She were wearing a dirty red dress and a red torn and stained hood hanged down her back. She must have found the cameo in the den cos she were wearing it on her chest. She looked lost and confused. I went to cry out to her but Ernie put a hand over me mouth even though it were gagged with the neckerchief. I kicked him and tried to escape but he were fat and strong. Then I seen Becky look in our direction. Her father suddenly came to life and he pointed the rifle at his daughter, telling her not to run. I were in a right state. I had no notion of what I were doing, except that I found meself running towards her, yelling out to her but of course, I were not making sense cos of me mouth gag. Becky were paralysed with astonishment. There were me running towards her, so were her father, screaming at her not to move or he would shoot her. Ernie were crying out, *No!* When he were close, Mr Carsons stopped in his tracks and aimed the rifle at his daughter, but she weren't looking at him only at me with murderous eyes. She started screaming that I had lied to her, that I had tricked her. I tore off me gag and told her I didn't trick her but she were spitting at me and snarling, calling me *liar, liar, liar* – oh, dearie, I have to make meself calm when I tell about this . . . oh dearie, it all comes back – Becky run at me, spitting and howling like some possessed, crazed animal, and threw herself on me. I seen her mouth open wide and I knew what she were going to do – she were so hysterical she were going to rip open me throat. I tried to push her away. Thank goodness Ernie were there, cos he grabbed her and threw her to the ground. Then, realising no one were holding her, she took off back to the den.

We ran after her. Then we stopped cos joining Becky outside the lair were a tiger – it were Corinna. But this were an old Corinna. Right scrawny she were, with her ribs showing and her muzzle white. Mr Carsons aimed his rifle at her. I could see the look in Corinna's eyes. She had a death wish. She were starving and old and Dave were dead cos of Mr Carsons. Were Mr Carsons going to put her out of her misery or kill her cos she had taken Becky from him? I don't know but as he pulled the trigger Becky jumped in front of Corinna to protect her. There were a shot and the whole valley echoed it. Becky shooked for a moment and then fell on her back in the snow. Blood were seeping from her chest and staining the snow red. She had her eyes closed. I knew for certain she were dead. Mr Carsons dropped his rifle and fell onto his knees in the snow. I were in such a state of shock that I were paralysed. All I could do were to stare at her. Ernie were crying softly, *No, no, no!* Mr Carsons were howling in agony like an animal caught in a steel trap. He crawled through the snow to her and cradled her, rocking back and forth like a baby. I noticed Corinna hadn't moved. She were staring at Becky and she knew Becky were dead.

Night were coming and I heard Ernie say, *Time to go home.* There were no other words to say. Mr Carsons wrapped his dead daughter's body in a blanket and roped her to his horse. I sat with Ernie on his horse. I still didn't believe Becky were dead. Even looking at her tied up like a bundle of clothes to her father's horse couldn't make me believe me she were gone. We rode off in silence. I looked back and saw Corinna staring at the bloodstained snow and then looking back at me. She seemed awfully weary and I knew she wanted to die and die she would soon, very soon.

We were all so knackered that during the four-day ride back to Mr Carsons's farm, we said barely a word. It were enough that we had the strength just to remain on the horses.

I s'pose I have to laugh rather than cry cos the reason Becky went back to the den were cos of Ernie's soft nature of giving her the ambergris that brought back all those memories for her. I reckon it must have took her six days of non-stop walking to make her way back to the lair. She made it to the den but I weren't there. It were only a sick and starving Corinna. Then not too long afterwards she heard me singing to her. It were no wonder she thought I were playing a trick on her.

We buried Becky on the farm with only Ernie as a mourner besides me and Mr Carsons. It were a sunny day. She would have liked that. I were hollowed out with grief, but Mr Carsons were even worse. He stayed in bed when he should have been up and working and he moved through the house like the living dead – he were a ghost but didn't know it yet. There were no spirit or soul in him any more. I saw a death wish like Corinna's in his eyes. Ernie must have seen it too cos he stayed on the farm caring for us, but Mr Carsons wouldn't eat. He were just waiting for death to come and get him but maybe death were taking too long and Mr Carsons were too impatient cos one night as me and

Ernie were sitting on the back porch we heard a shot from the bedroom. Mr Carsons had finally given up waiting for death so he decided to go and meet death himself.

We buried him next to Becky. Ernie said he would care for me. I returned to Hobart to live with him. Me grief for Becky were deep and long-lasting. Ernie recorded me talking and singing, but only for short bits cos that's all the cylinders would take. I were growing into me teenage years with Ernie and he were growing old, not so much cos of real age but cos he were becoming fatter and he found breathing and even walking a trial at times. He knew he should take off weight but he said he couldn't. *I am a weak-willed man*, he said to me more than once. He tried to teach me to speak better but I only got as good as this. I never did learn to write or read properly. He were scared of what would happen to me if he died, so he wanted me to be able to earn money. He thought I should go back to whaling but there were few whalers now cos the whales were becoming less and less. He got me a job as a housemaid in a large house at the bottom of Mount Wellington. It were hard work and the woman of the household would yell at me, calling me *simple. Simple Hannah.*

I used to visit Ernie cos he were me only friend. One day he didn't answer the door. He used to lock it cos he were afeared someone were going to steal all his cylinders and recording equipment. I crept in through a back window and seen him face down in the corridor. I heaved him over. He had a terrible look of fear on his face. Like he'd seen or thought something dreadful before he died.

The rest of me life has passed without big things happening to me. I were a housekeeper and housemaid for several years. I hated the work I were doing but I knew I could do nothing else. I saved every penny I could cos before he died Ernie had made sure I were the owner of me mother and father's property. I thought if I saved up enough I could fix up the house without having to work for anyone, and live simply by meself. I never had a boy or man in me life, nor anyone else. How could I explain to them what I been through? Who would understand? Only Becky knew. I had me dogs, me chooks, me pigs, me freedom. There were a general store seven miles down the track and it were an easy walk there. The people of the town think I'm strange and now I'm old some children think I'm a witch.

I never went into Hobart again after visiting Becky's school although I heard there were a zoo that held the last Tasmanian tigers. I didn't believe they were the last because out here I used to see them, smell them or I seen their dung. They were cautious of me cos I'm a human and I stayed me distance but sometimes of a night I'd sit on the verandah and see them moving silently through the bush. Bit by bit, over the years there were less and less tigers til now I can honestly say I haven't seen one for 'bout five years. Maybe they've gone further inland cos of the number of people shifting into the area – I want to believe that, I got to, cos tigers saved me life and Becky's.

I never felt alone cos I sensed the spirit of Becky all round me. Every night I have the same dream. It's not quite a dream cos it seems real to me. I find meself back in the bush on a sunny day. A girl comes out of the woods with two tigers. They stand and wait for me. It's Becky, Dave and Corinna. I walk towards them with a feeling of great happiness. We are together again. I grab Becky's hand and we walk back into that forest with a tiger either side of us. I wake up happy cos I know that they are waiting for me to join them. And I will.

Author's Note

Into that Forest is based on a story I wrote with Vincent Ward, originally titled 'Hannah and Rebecca'. Eventually we decided to work on other projects but Vincent urged me over a decade ago to turn it into a novel. The novel I have written is very different in many respects from the original; however, at its heart it is still the story of Hannah and Rebecca and the two Tasmanian tigers.

The novel has a factual basis in that I have been to Tasmania many times and consulted a number of sources, including the following:

Q. Beresford and G. Bailey, *Search for the Tasmanian Tiger*, Blubber Head Press, Hobart, 1981

Maureen Brooks and Joan Ritchie, *Tassie Terms: a glossary of Tasmanian Words*, Oxford University Press, Melbourne, 1985

E.R. Guiler, *Thylacine: the Tragedy of the Tasmanian Tiger*, Oxford University Press, Melbourne, 1985

E.R. Guiler, *The Tasmanian Tiger in Pictures*, St David's Park Publishing, Hobart, 1991

Charles Maclean, *The Wolf Children*, Allen Lane, London, 1977

Herman Melville, *Moby-Dick*, various editions

Robert Paddle, *The Last Tasmanian Tiger: the History and Extinction of the Thylacine*, Cambridge University Press, Melbourne, 2000

I also consulted *Australian Geographic* and other magazines, plus various articles on early gramophones.